First Love

OAKVILLE SERIES: BOOK ONE

First Love

Oakville Series: Book One

Kathy-Jo Reinhart

Kathy-Jo Reinhart
First Love (Oakville Series #1)
© 2014, Kathy-Jo Reinhart
Self-publishing
(kathyjoreinhart.com)

Interior designed and formatted by E.M. Tippetts Book Designs

I would like to dedicate this book to my grandparents. They were two of the most wonderful people I have ever had the privilege of knowing. My whole life they were always my biggest supporters. Without their influence, love and support I wouldn't be who I am today. For that I will always be grateful. I miss you both every day.

Prologue

Amber
Six Years ago

I HAVE BEEN sitting around in my bedroom for most of the day. The local radio station is giving away concert tickets and backstage passes for the band Breaking Benjamin. You have to be the tenth caller. My boyfriend, Kyle, loves this band. He would be thrilled if I won these tickets. The concert is in Miami three weeks from now. As luck would have it, we are set to leave in two weeks for Miami. Kyle and I are going to be living together while we go to college. We want to get settled in our new apartment before we start our first year at the University of Miami, so we are going about a month early. It was perfect. Now, all I had to do was win the damn things. I had a cell phone and landline, using both to call. So far, I have been every caller number but ten.

We have known each other since we were toddlers. Since I was very young, I have known that I loved him. I just never said anything to him. I was always afraid he didn't feel the same for me. When we were in ninth grade, he told me he had always felt the same way. We have been a couple ever since. I know we are still young, but there is no doubt in my heart that he is my soul mate. We plan on getting married

1

someday. He is the only guy I have ever dated, but I couldn't imagine wanting anyone else.

"Be our tenth caller now to win a pair of tickets and back stage passes to see Breaking Benjamin," the DJ said over the radio.

I picked up the phones and hit redial. Busy signals. I continued to hang up and redial. I really wanted to win this. Unfortunately, it didn't look like I was going to make it this time, either. They had to have gotten the tenth caller by now. I tried one more time, just in case. I hit redial on both phones, again. A busy signal sounded through the landline right away, so I hung it up. I still had my cell phone to my ear and, this time, the call was going through. After four rings, someone finally answered the phone. My heart was pounding so hard in my chest. *Please let me win. Please let me win.* I took a deep breath and waited for the person on the other end to speak.

"You are caller number ten! What's your name?" I recognized the voice of the DJ I had been listening to all day.

"Amber," I said with a shaky voice. I had won! Kyle wasn't going to believe this.

"Well, Amber, you just won tickets and passes for Breaking Benjamin. Hang on the line and we will get your information."

I waited on hold for a minute or so before another voice came on the line. They took down my name and phone number, telling me I could pick up my tickets any time from the radio station. I decided I was going now to get them. I changed my clothes and headed out to my car, a brand new Camaro SS. I have always loved muscle cars and this was the ultimate one, a graduation gift from my grandparents. I got in, cranked her up, and headed to the radio station.

After I got the tickets and passes from the radio station, I was so anxious to see the look on his face, I decided to go straight to Kyle's. As I was driving to his house, my phone beeped saying I had a text. When I stopped at a red light, I looked at my phone.

> **Kyle:** *Just got home from band practice. Gonna take a shower. Call ya later. Luv ya.*

I didn't have a chance to text back because the light turned green. I would be at his house in a couple minutes anyway, I'll just surprise him when he gets out of the shower. As I drove along, my mind was starting to drift. I kept picturing Kyle's perfect body, all wet from the shower. Lucky damn water. He is absolute perfection from head to toe: six-foot-three with the perfect amount of muscles in all the right areas, and dark brown hair that is the perfect mix of rocker and boy next door. It isn't very long, but it always looks disheveled. Kind of like he just rolled out of bed. And, the best part...his eyes. He has the most beautiful cobalt blue eyes. I could gaze into them for hours. Suddenly, I knew exactly what I wanted him to do in order to thank me for the tickets.

I pulled into his driveway and parked my car. His parents were out of town this weekend, so we would have the whole house to ourselves. The front door was unlocked. No surprise there. This is a very small town, no one really worries about locking doors. I walked into the house. I could hear the shower running as I walked toward the hallway. *Should I slip into the shower with him? Or, should I get naked and wait in his bed?* I decided to wait in his bed.

When I opened the door to his bedroom, my heart shattered. Nora Lawson was laying there wearing nothing but a shit eating grin on her face. Fucking bitch! I wanted to puke, scream, and cry. I just couldn't decide which to do first. I heard the shower turn off and I ran out of the house, dropping the tickets to floor as I went. There was no way in hell I could face him. It was bad enough that she had seen my devastation.

When I got home, I asked my grandparents to tell Kyle I wasn't feeling well if he called or came over. Once I got to my room, I locked my door and fell to the bed. My heart felt like it was actually breaking. I have never hurt so badly in my life, nor cried so hard. I can't believe he betrayed me like that. With Nora, of all people. Eventually, I cried myself to sleep.

I spent the next day and a half crying and avoiding Kyle. I didn't want to see him. I was too hurt and upset. He couldn't say anything that would make me feel any better. He cheated on me. There was no excuse for it. It was obvious I wasn't enough for him. I couldn't bear to hear him say it to my face. Why would he make all of these plans with me if he wanted someone else? I had to have missed the signs. I had my head too far up my ass because I was so in love. What the fuck do I know about love? Obviously, nothing. I do know that I will never put myself through this kind of pain again. I had to get away from here. Away from him.

I had a very long talk with my grandparents, who have raised me since I was two. I told them I had changed my mind about Miami. They were pretty surprised, to say the least. The big shocker came when I told them I was going alone. They loved Kyle. I didn't tell them what Kyle had done. I didn't want them to hate him because our relationship went south. After all, he thought of my grandparents as his own. He never knew his own and mine treated him just like a grandson. I told them that I needed to do this on my own and Kyle didn't understand that. I made them promise not to tell him where I was going. I knew they weren't too thrilled with that idea, but would do what I asked of them.

After my talk with my grandparents, I went to my room to pack. I decided to leave first thing in the morning. As much as I hate to leave them, I have to get away from Florida. I had applied to Georgia State University as a back-up school and I think going to Georgia would be the best thing. I only packed what I absolutely needed. I couldn't fit a whole lot in my car, anyway. As soon as I packed, I quickly loaded it in my car. Kyle had been calling and texting like crazy. The more I ignored him, the worse it got. He had even come by a couple times today, but my grandma told him I was sick. I just couldn't understand why he seemed so worried about getting a hold of me. He couldn't really love me if he was cheating on me, so why does he care? Something doesn't add up, but my heart hurts too much to listen. Maybe I was being a coward by leaving, and I am probably going to regret not getting an explanation, but I'm just too broken right now to care.

My alarm clock went off at 5 A.M. I wanted to make sure I got to Atlanta early enough to find a good hotel. Tomorrow, I would be apartment hunting. I also didn't want to run into Kyle. I dressed comfortably for my nine hour drive in yoga pants and a t-shirt. I grabbed my duffel bag off my bed and headed toward my door. I turned and took another long look around my room. I am really going to miss this place. I quickly close the door before I start crying.

In the kitchen, there is a thermos of coffee and a letter from grandma. I said my goodbyes last night. I knew it would be a big cry fest this morning if I didn't. My grandparents went to Georgia often, so it's not like I would never see them. I opened the note and began reading it.

> *Dear Amber,*
> *I know you are hurting right now. I wish there was something I could do to ease that hurt for you. As always,*

you are a very strong, independent, and stubborn young woman. I may be old, but I am not senile. At least, not yet. I can see that this has something to do with Kyle. I am not going to pry. If you want to talk, you will come to me. I will say one thing, though. Love like you both have comes only once in life. Time apart may not be a bad thing for either of you. It will be a good chance for you both to grow, also a chance for you both to realize how much you really do love one another. You are both young and bound to make mistakes. One day, you will realize that the love you have for each other is more important than anything else. You will eventually be able to forgive, because that is who you are. I have never met anyone more forgiving than you. Trust yourself.

Call us when you get to Atlanta and maybe a couple times along the way, just so we know you are safe. We will make sure to come see you often. You are so special to us, the most important person in our lives. We love you so much. Have a safe trip.
Love Always,
Grandma and Grandpa

I wiped my tears and put the letter in my bag. I love that woman dearly, but the pain in my heart made it very difficult to even think about forgiveness right now. I headed out to my car. I took another long look at the house that held so many happy memories for me before I got in and drove toward my new life. Far away from the man I love who has ripped my heart into shreds.

Kyle

I WAVED goodbye to the guys as I got into my truck. We had just finished band practice. I started this band when I was in eighth grade. We play covers from hard rock and metal bands and we're pretty good. Our only gigs consist of birthday parties and the occasional house party, but that doesn't matter to me. I am not looking to get famous or become a rock star. Someday, I'd like to have my own bar and restaurant, then I could play whenever I felt like it.

Normally, Amber comes to every practice with me. Today she said she had something to do for her grandmother. I really hope she's finished by now, I can't wait any longer to see her. The guys are always teasing me, saying I'm whipped because I spend so much time with her. I'm not whipped; I'm just head over heels in love with her. I have been in love with her for as long as I can remember. Hell, I loved her long before I even knew what love was.

I parked my truck in the driveway and went into my house. My parents went to visit my aunt in Tampa this weekend, so I had the whole house to myself. That could come in very handy later if Amber wanted to stop by. I shoot her a quick text to let her know I am home. Maybe she will have the same ideas I'm having.

I waited a couple minutes for a reply. When I didn't get one, I jumped in the shower. While I stood under the hot spray of the water, I couldn't help but think about Amber. She is the most beautiful girl I have ever seen. She is slim, but not too skinny. She has the most perfect tits. And, her ass, I can't keep my hands off of it. I catch guys checking out her ass all the time. Her eyes, though, the most beautiful shade of chocolate brown, were my favorite attribute. I could get lost in her eyes. There was just something about them that was mesmerizing. At a whole foot shorter than me, five-foot-three, I couldn't help but tease her. I love it, though.

I thought I heard the front door slam. Maybe Amber came over after all. I quickly rinsed off and got out of the shower. I dried off and wrapped the towel around my waist. I couldn't wait to see her. I felt myself harden at the thought of being close to her. I walked out of the bathroom and into my bedroom, shocked to find Nora Lawson naked in my bed. It definitely wasn't who I was expecting it to be. For the last four years, she has been trying to get me to sleep with her. This, however, was a whole new low. Even for her.

"What the fuck are you doing in here?" I yelled. I wanted to grab her and throw her out of my house. Unfortunately, I think she would have taken that as a come on.

"Ah, what's the matter, Kyle? You were very happy to see me when you first walked in," she said, staring at my crotch.

Too bad, the second my eyes landed on this bitch my dick shriveled right up as if I had jumped into a pool of ice water.

"Believe me, I wasn't happy to see you. You need to get your clothes on and leave now. I have told you before, I want *nothing* to do with you!" I grabbed a pair of jeans and went back to the bathroom to get dressed. I had to get her the fuck out of here. I walked out of the bathroom just as Nora was leaving.

"I have a feeling you are going to change your mind about me, Kyle. When your straight-laced girlfriend dumps your ass, you know where to find me," she said with a smirk. She knew something that I didn't. I wasn't in the mood to play games. I just wanted her gone.

"Don't hold your breath, Nora." She started to walk away. "On second thought, maybe you should hold your breath," I said with my own smirk.

"Fuck you, Kyle Connor!" she spat as she slammed the front door.

Thank God she was gone. I threw on some socks, boots, and a t-shirt. As I was walking to the front door, I noticed an envelope on the floor. I picked it up. My name was typed on the front. I opened it up and was floored. There were two tickets and two backstage passes to see Breaking Benjamin. I love that band! Where the hell did these come from? This envelope wasn't here when I came in. Then again, neither was Nora.

I looked at my phone, Amber still hadn't replied to my text. That was strange. She usually responded right away. An uneasy feeling settled in my stomach. Something wasn't right. I tried calling Amber's cell phone. Straight to voice mail. The only time it did that was when she ignored the call. Why is she avoiding me? On a knee-jerk reaction, I decide I'm not going to wonder for long. I grab my keys and head out the door. I'm not waiting to find out.

On the way to Amber's house, I called three more times. All three times it went straight to voice mail. Something was definitely wrong, but what? I drove a little faster. I don't know why, but a feeling of dread washed over me. I felt it even worse as I parked my truck in Amber's driveway. Her car was there. She was home. I walked up to the front door. Before I could knock, the door opened and Ima, Amber's grandma, walked out, closing the door behind her.

"What's going on, Grams?" I asked, my voice trembling. My knees felt weak. I sat on the wooden bench, which sat next to the front door. She looked torn. I knew whatever she was about to say was going to be something Amber told her to say. Gene and Ima have been like grandparents to me since I was only a few years old. They are the only grandparents I have ever known. But, Amber came first, and I understood that. I always put her first, too. Ima rested her hand on mine, a sad smile tweaking her lips as she sat next to me.

"Nothing is going on, dear. She has the flu. She's just not up to any company right now."

"Did I do something wrong? I don't understand why she's avoiding me all of a sudden. Everything was fine this morning." I was starting to sound like a whiney little bitch.

"Honestly, Kyle, I don't know. She won't tell us anything, either. Whatever it is, I am sure it will blow over. Just give her some space. By tomorrow, or the next day, it will probably all be forgotten." She kissed the top of head as she stood up. "Don't worry. I'm sure everything will be fine." She patted my shoulder and went inside. I got up and went to my truck, turning to look up to her window. I guess I was hoping to see her, but I didn't. I got in my truck and left.

For the next two days, I called Amber, time and time again, only to get voicemail. I left so many messages, eventually her mailbox was full. When I couldn't leave any more messages, I sent a text every hour. Still, no response. My emotions kept flip-flopping back and forth. One minute, I was so angry I was breaking everything in sight; the next, I was crying like a baby, broken. If only she'd talk to me so I knew what the fuck I did. I can't fix it if I don't know what the problem is. I couldn't take any more. I stayed away for two days, two agonizing days. I had to know what I did wrong. This time, she was going to talk to me.

That feeling of dread was back as I pulled into the driveway. Her car was gone. It's not like she would have went very far. I'll just wait; I don't care how long it takes. Again, before I could knock the door opened and out came Ima. Shit. She looked like she was about to tell me my dog died. This wasn't going to be good. My heart felt like it was in a vice grip. Time to man up.

"I'm not leaving until she comes back. She needs to tell me what the problem is so I can fix it and we can move on." She moved closer to me and placed an arm around me.

"Kyle. She left this morning, she's not coming back."

"What do you mean she's not coming back? Today? Tomorrow? Next week?" I looked at her, wanting an explanation. At the same time, I didn't. I'm positive I'm not going to like it.

"She's not coming back at all. Ever. She wanted me to tell you it was over."

"I don't understand. Why? What did I do? Where did she go?" Tears started to fall, but I didn't care. Why did she leave me? Why wouldn't she at least tell me goodbye?

"I don't know why. She still wouldn't tell us. I can't tell you where she is. She made us promise. I'm so sorry. I know how much the two of you love each other."

"She doesn't love me! If she loved me she wouldn't just leave without a single word. Not even a goodbye." I fell to the ground crying. Ima followed and wrapped her arms around me. She must have stayed there with me for a good hour and a half. In my truck, on my way home, I made a promise to myself. No fucking way was I ever getting hurt by another woman again. Amber was my first and last relationship.

CHAPTER
One

Amber

I WAS DRIVING home through downtown Atlanta. I usually spent the whole day volunteering at the youth center, but I left before lunch. I called my fiancé, Daniel, at his office to see how his morning in court went and his secretary told me he went home early because he wasn't feeling well. I thought that was strange. He never gets sick and he was fine when he left this morning.

When I moved to Atlanta six years ago, I was a heartbroken mess. I could barely function for the first year. I only left my tiny, one bedroom apartment to go to classes, the library, and the coffee shop across the street from my apartment.

One evening, walking into the coffee shop in my normal zombie-like state, I was quickly pulled from my stupor. I slammed into something hard, a wet burning sensation spilling down the front of me, followed by a very sexy male voice yelling, "Oh, shit ... are you okay?" I look up to see a gorgeous man with short, jet black hair and the most beautiful brown eyes I think I have ever seen. Normally, I like blue eyes. But, these eyes were almost hypnotic with long, thick lashes. After I got over my embarrassment from not only running into him and spilling his coffee all over the two of us, but also from obviously drooling all over him, I was finally able to speak.

"I am so sorry ... I wasn't paying attention." Oh God, his smile might be better than his eyes. His low chuckle snapped me back to reality. "Let me replace your coffee for you, I feel terrible." He looked at me and flashed that damn smile again.

"Sure, on two conditions. One, you join me. Two, we don't wear them," he teased, laughing. From that night on, we became friends. He was funny, charming, sweet, and sexy as hell, but the last thing on my mind was putting my heart out there again.

We would go to dinner, movies, or just hang out at home. By taking me out and doing things, he helped pull me out of my depression. After about a year and a half, he told me he was in love with me. I was shocked. I honestly didn't think he felt anything more for me than friendship. I knew I cared for him, but I still wasn't ready for a relationship and I was honest with him. Again, he was his normal, wonderful self. He acted like nothing happened and we continued our friendship as it was.

About two years ago, he brought it up again. At this point, I felt that maybe it was time. He had been so patient with me and slowly gained my trust. Things with Daniel Ford were easy and comfortable. My heart was safe.

About a year ago, when Daniel completed law school, he asked me to marry him. I accepted. We moved in together about six months ago.

I tried to call his cell phone to see if he needed anything before I left work. It went to voicemail. I pull up in front of our townhouse and head inside. I don't want to wake him, so I close the front door quietly behind me. As soon as I turn around, I start to feel a little ill myself. A trail of clothes led from the living room down the hall to the bedroom. I feel frozen in place, my feet refusing to carry me forward. After what seems like hours, but was only minutes, I force myself to follow the trail of discarded clothing. I know what I'm going to find at the end of the trail, but I need to see it with my own eyes to believe it was happening. The range of emotions playing through my head made it throb: anger, hurt, sadness. I try to think of any signs that I missed; anything that may have clued me in to his cheating. I actually start to wonder if there was something I lacked that made him do this. How pathetic ... I was not one of those girls. He was going to be lucky to make it out of here with his balls still attached. He knew what I went through before I met him. Christ, he waited four fucking years to date me.

A loud moan assaulted my ears as I got closer to our bedroom. The door is cracked, so I slowly look inside. My stomach is twisted in knots and I can feel the burn of bile making its way up my throat as soon as I see them. I gather myself up ... I may have been a coward once, but I'll be damned if I am one again. I walk into the room as calmly as possible, stand at the foot of the bed, and clear my throat. "Excuse me ... could you two please finish up here so I can start packing my shit," I say as sweetly as possible. I refuse to cry over another cheating asshole. The whore bag was looking at me like *I* was the one in her bed fucking *her* fiancé. I really want to grab her by her bleach-blonde extensions and throw her boney ass out into the front lawn, naked. Daniel was quick to jump off of her and head toward me. I threw my hands up to stop him. "Put some clothes on and get your whore out of my bed," I say without even a crack in my voice. I'm proud of myself. I don't even feel like crying. Weird. Maybe I'm just too pissed off.

"Who are you calling a whore?" she screeches as she jumps out of the bed, wrapping the sheet around herself.

I slowly looked her up and down as I walk up to her and say, "You are the one in MY house, in MY bed, fucking MY fiancé! To me, that spells whore." By now, I have her backed up against the wall and she's starting to look a little worried. *Good.* "You have five minutes to get your clothes on and get your ass out of my sight. I am not above throwing you out myself." With that, she got her ass in gear and headed out of the room. Maybe she wasn't as dumb as she looked.

"Amber, honey, let me explain ... it's not what it looks like," Daniel pleads. I spin around to face him and just start laughing. Honestly, did he really just say that?

"It looked like you were fucking her," I say, matter-of-factly.

He starts to speak, but I shoot him a looked that shut him up. I start laughing, again. "Let me guess ... both of you just happened to lose your clothes and she tripped. You tried to catch her, but fell on top of her and your dick accidently slipped inside? Really, Daniel? Do you think I am that stupid? How could it possibly not be what it looked like? At least have the balls to not make excuses." I shake my head and head for the closet to get my suitcases. I calmly start packing everything I have.

"I really am sorry. I didn't mean to hurt you." I can see that he is sorry by the look on his face. Whether it was for getting caught or actually cheating, who knows. My guess is a mixture of both. I have known in my heart since I met Daniel that I loved him. Was it the earth stopping, can't breathe without him, kind of love? No. I had that once and I don't think I will ever have it again. But, I thought my heart was safe with him.

"You knew I went through this before and how much it broke me; how hard it was for me to trust you. The whole time you knew you were just going to do the same thing but figured you were smarter and wouldn't get caught. I am pissed, more so at myself for being so stupid... for ever trusting you in the first place!"

He had nothing to say. Really, what could he say? Nothing could change it. I start to realize that this felt nothing like the last time. I am sad, most definitely angry, and a little humiliated, but I am not crushed. I was devastated when I found out about Kyle. I should be just as devastated now. Like a ton of bricks, it hit me. I never loved Daniel enough to marry him. I love him as a friend. I was too scared after Kyle to put my heart on the line again. Daniel was there. And, because I didn't have those deep feelings for him, I was safe. I am no better than Daniel.

As I'm packing my clothes, I have to figure out what I want to do. I realize that I need to go back home. Home is where I really belong and the only place I was ever happy. Although I had no family left, I still love that small town. Too bad Kyle isn't there anymore. Last I heard, he was in California, following his dream of becoming rock star.

Daniel helps me load everything into my car. I guess it's the least he could do. Before I get in, I take my engagement ring off my finger and put it in his palm. "I never should have said yes in the first place. I am sorry for that." I kiss his cheek and say goodbye.

During the nine-hour drive to Oakville, Florida, a very small town near the Everglades where I grew up, I can't help but think about my life before I left. When I was two, my parents died in a car accident. My father's parents, my only living relatives, raised me. I had a wonderful childhood and loved my grandparents dearly. After I moved to Atlanta, I didn't go home much, but they came to visit me often. They had asked a few times what had happened to make me leave as quickly as I did, but I never told them what I saw. I didn't want them worrying that I was making life decisions solely based on a broken heart. Though, that's what I did. My heart was definitely broken and I was a mess. It's a miracle I passed the first year of college.

About six months after I left, Kyle stopped asking them about me. Within a year, he was off to L.A. When we made our plans to go to college, I couldn't help but wonder if I was holding him back from his dreams. I would have supported anything he wanted to do, but he always said that being famous and singing full time was not the lifestyle he wanted. He wanted to own a restaurant where he could play his music on the weekends. He said it would be like having the best of both worlds. I guess it was all a lie, just like all the times he told me how much he loved me.

A year ago, my grandpa passed away. Luckily, I was able to be here for a couple of weeks with him before he died. They had waited a long time to tell me he had cancer because they didn't want to worry me, afraid I would drop everything to come home. Of course I would have dropped everything to come home, anything to spend more time with them. Two days after he passed away, Grandma went to sleep one night and never woke up. They were married for over sixty years. It didn't surprise me that one couldn't live without the other. They had a lot of hard times, but always got through it together.

They had the kind of love that we all dream of having. It was the kind I thought I had once. When the other person steps into the room and everything stands still. Your heart rate picks up to the point it feels like it is going to break through your chest. When you are apart, they are always running through your mind and you can't wait to be with them again. The kind of love that can make your knees weak. Yeah, I felt that once ... it's just too bad Kyle didn't.

My grandparents left me the house, land, and enough money to keep me comfortable for a very long time. In order to thank them and make them proud, a lot of my time was spent volunteering at shelters and youth centers trying to help as many people as I could.

I turn off the main road onto the mile long dirt road leading to the house. The sun is just starting to rise, unveiling the green grass and old oak trees. I always forget how beautiful it is here. As the house came into view, I couldn't help but smile. It made me think of my grandparents, Kyle, and all of the good times I had growing up. It also made my chest ache; I could feel the tears welling up in my eyes.

I park the car in the driveway and get out, stretching with a long groan. The house is a huge two-story, old, white Victorian with a gigantic wrap-around porch. After my grandparents passed away, I had a few things updated. Mr. and Mrs. Thompson, my dear neighbors, watched over the renovations for me. The backyard is still my favorite place, though.

Surrounding a massive, built-in, stone BBQ pit is a large wooden deck with a luscious view of Azaleas and roses in every possible color. My grandmother loved her flowers. In the far back corner, there is a stone path that leads through a cluster of trees to the most beautiful pond. I would sit by that pond for hours when I was younger. Sitting on the deck with a drink sounds like heaven right about now.

I walk up the steps onto the porch, unlock the front door, and step through the doorway. To the left of the foyer is a large kitchen that I had updated with black granite countertops, cherry cabinets, and new stainless appliances. I couldn't wait to start using this room; it was perfect. I had all the hardwood flooring replaced throughout the entire house and new tile put in the kitchen. Off of the kitchen there is a formal dining room with a beautiful crystal chandelier in the center of the old, dark, carved wooden table. Across from the kitchen was a spacious living room with a corner stone fireplace and a large bay window looking out into the front yard. There was also a den off of the living room and a small bathroom. The entire house had been painted inside and out. I headed upstairs to check out the other changes. The bathroom in the hallway between the three guest bedrooms had been updated with new tile flooring and a more modern sink, toilet, and walk-in shower. I walk to the end of the hall to the master bedroom. I had put in a large fireplace which added to the already spectacular room. Not that I will use it much in Florida; I just love the look of a warm, inviting fireplace. There is a massive four-poster bed at one end and a large window that looks over the beautiful flower gardens in the backyard at the other. In front of the window and fireplace is a sitting area with an oversized armchair, ottoman, and side table. I can just picture myself curled up in the chair reading a good book. Next, I look in the master bathroom. A double sink had been installed next to a large garden tub. A separate walk-in, glass shower was the perfect focal point. As I was walking back down the stairs, my stomach began to growl. To the fridge, I went. When I pull the doors open, I'm surprised to find it well-stocked. Mrs. Thompson will be getting something special to thank her for that. I start a pot of coffee and make a couple pieces of toast. After I finish my breakfast, I begin unpacking my car.

Kyle

WE JUST finished playing at a huge bar in Tallahassee. The guys and I headed up to the bar for a couple beers. Of course, by the time we made it there we were surrounded by half the women in the bar. Back in the day, when we played in L.A., none of us would think twice about hooking up with one of them, sometimes two. Now, things are different. Paul, our drummer, has a steady girlfriend. Marcus, our bass player, is married. Angel, our lead guitarist, well, nothing has really changed for him. Case in point, he is heading to the bathroom with two sexy brunettes following behind him. I was just like that for quite a few years. After a while, though, it got old. There was only one girl I ever really loved. Even after six years, it still hurts to think about her. Though she is probably married by now and long over me, I cleaned up my act a few months ago, anyway. I would never be able to move on if I kept going the way I was with a different woman every night.

A beautiful blonde came up to me and sat on my lap. She was giving me a look that said I could take her and do anything I pleased. Unfortunately, I didn't want her.

"Sorry, doll. Not tonight." I gently nudged her off my lap.

"You have no idea what kind of pleasure I could give you," she purred. There was no doubt in my mind of the things she could do. I just wasn't interested.

"Really, I'm not interested." I turned away from her and took a pull from my beer.

"Oh...are the two of you together?" she asked, motioning between Paul and me. I spit the mouthful of beer I had out over the bar. Grabbing the towel that was laying on the bar, I wiped up my mess.

"No we aren't together. I'm just not interested in you or any other women in this bar tonight." She gave me a nasty look and stomped away. No wonder I never used to say no. It was so much easier to find a dark corner to fuck them and then send them on their way. So much easier than this shit.

"You're thinking about her again, aren't you?" Paul asked with an amused look on his face. He loved to give me shit when it came to Amber.

"I can't seem to think of much else lately." I shook my head and drank my beer.

"Why don't you try to find her again? She could still be just as hung up on you. Anything is possible. Plus, I have got to meet the girl that has had you tied in knots for six years."

"You're lucky you're a good drummer," I joked. "She is probably happily married and has long forgotten about my ass by now. She left me, remember?" I said with a chuckle.

I would give anything to have her back again. I went to find her once, but it didn't go so well. She was with someone else, so I came back home. Maybe when I get back home I'll try looking her up again. Just to see if she is still with that guy from Atlanta.

"Holly sent me a text. She hired a new waitress today," Paul said

"Great. Someone else to keep Angel from fucking and pissing off."

"Maybe this one's not his type."

"Yeah right!" I laughed. "Every women is his type." We both burst out laughing.

CHAPTER
Two

Amber

TWO WEEKS have passed since I arrived back in Oakville. Daniel has tried to call a few times, but I just let it go to voicemail. All the messages are the same: he's sorry and wants to make sure I am okay. I don't hate him; we both did each other wrong. I should have never agreed to marry him in the first place. I didn't love him enough to spend the rest of my life with him. That wasn't fair to him. Maybe deep down he knew it too, and that's why he looked elsewhere. I eventually texted him back, telling him I made it okay and that I was doing fine. I also told him that I thought it would be best if we didn't talk to each other ... at least for a while. A clean break was for the best.

I really meant it when I said I was okay. Aside from the fact that two weeks of being in this town has triggered so many memories. It was driving me a more than a little crazy, especially realizing that after six years, I am still very much in love with Kyle Connor. No other man will probably ever compare. I have no idea where he is, who he's with, or, worse yet, if he would ever want me again. It's not like he's going to come riding up on a white horse and sweep me off my feet. He has had six years to do that. Even if he did, do I really want to be with someone who cheated on me? We were just kids; it's not like we were mature or knew anything about relationships. It was not the same as what happened with Daniel. Or was it? Hell, I don't even know. The only thing I do know is I can't seem to get Kyle out of my head.

I had everything unpacked and put away within the first day of being back. I made a list of all the things I needed around the house and did all my shopping. I had also invited the Thompson's over for dinner as a thank you for all their help over the last year, and so I could try out the new kitchen on someone other than myself. It was as awesome to cook in as I thought it was going to be. I read three books and polished off too many bottles of wine by myself. Needless to say, I'm getting a little bored. I need to get out of this house, get a job, do something that will keep me busy.

When I was in high school I waitressed at The Shack, a bar and grill a few miles away. I always enjoyed working there. It was really the only hang-out in town for the high school crowd. A large room set up in the back with pool tables, dart boards, and a few video games was the perfect spot to pass the hours on a Friday night. The diner was the only other place to eat in town, so business was always steady. Deciding that it would be fun to work there again, getting to know some of the new people in town or even see some of the people I grew up with, I rush to get ready. It won't hurt to see if they are hiring. I take a quick shower and throw on some skinny jeans, a white t-shirt, and sneakers as I toss my hair up in a ponytail and head for the door.

I pull up in front of The Shack, instantly noticing that it is now called KC's Bar & Grille. The outside still looks the same; a wooden, rustic-looking building on the water with a large deck covered in tables jutting out from the building for outdoor eating. A long wooden dock led out over the water with boat slips to tie to, offering diners a beautiful view of the lake. Typical neon beer signs hang in the windows along with a sign advertising Mondays and Wednesdays as karaoke nights. I love karaoke. I have a decent voice and enjoy singing. Though, I usually need a couple of drinks to loosen me up a little. Friday and Saturday nights are reserved for live music.

I walk through the front doors, pleasantly surprised at how nice it is inside. The place looks a lot classier than it used to. The new owners have definitely updated the interior. The bar is u-shaped, located prominently in the center of the room. Off to the right is a raised stage area with a dance floor. Behind the bar is a long rectangle window with a counter leading back to the kitchen. To the left, all along the walls, booths are set up and tables sit in the center of the floor. Two neon signs hang on the far, back, left corner above an arched doorway. One sign read: POOL TABLES, and the other brightly announced: RESTROOMS. Only a few people sat eating at the tables and booths. I slide up on a stool at the bar. The woman behind the bar is a tall red head with beautiful teal eyes.

"Hi, I'm Holly, what can I get for ya?" she asks with a huge smile.

"Hey, I'm Amber. I'll have an Appletini, please." Yes, I know, typical girlie drink. But they are so good.

"I haven't seen you around before, did you just move to town or are you visiting?"

"I was born and raised here. I moved away six years ago for college and just moved back a couple weeks ago." She hands me my drink before getting called off to tend to one of the booths. I looked around and couldn't help but notice that she was the only one working. Maybe luck was on my side, after all. When she came back my way, I asked, "Holly, are you guys hiring waitresses right now?"

"Actually, yeah. Leslie quit yesterday, so I have been waitressing, bartending, and managing the place by myself. The owner, KC, and the usual bartender, Paul, go on the road with their band one month a year to play clubs all over the state. They won't be back for another three weeks. Are you looking for a job?"

"Yeah, I worked here before I moved away and I am going stir crazy just sitting at home alone all the time." The biggest smile lit up her face

"I think you are my new best friend. Can you start tomorrow?"

"Absolutely," I say, my smile matching hers. We sat and talked for a while. She and Paul, the usual bartender and drummer for the band Bleeding Hearts, have been dating for about six months.

"All of the boys in the band will make your panties wet with just a smile. But, I'll warn you now, KC is definitely the one to stay away from ... with exception to my man, that is." She gave me a wink. "What's wrong with KC?" I ask. Not that I'm looking for a man, I'm just curious. She looks like she is trying to decide what to tell me.

"I don't know the whole story, but I guess he got his heart broken a while back. He was seriously in love with this girl, ready to propose and everything, and she just took off, no goodbye or anything. Ever since, he hasn't been with the same girl longer than a night or two.

Don't get me wrong, as a friend and a boss he's a nice guy, but not boyfriend material. I think he's still waiting around for the girl who left him to come back."

Wow, that's kind of sad. "Well, you don't have to worry about that with me. The last thing on my mind is getting into any kind of relationship. The only two I've been in ended with both guys cheating, so I'm taking a break." Thankfully, she changed the subject to herself and I found that I really liked her. I think we are going to get along really well.

She had me fill out all the paperwork and introduced me to the cooks, Marty and Clark. Marty looked to be in his fifties. What little hair he does have is grey, and by the size of his belly, I could tell that he likes his beer and dislikes exercise. He seems a little grumpy, but Holly says he's a real sweetheart once he warms up to you. I guess we will have to see if that rings true. He has a wife named Anna and two kids. His son, Matthew, is twenty and in college and his daughter, Makenna, is sixteen and a sophomore in high school.

Clark is younger, early thirties by the looks of him. Not very tall, maybe five-foot-six, but he is very hot. He has brown hair cut short in a military style with large, espresso brown eyes. When I am ready to start dating again, I think I may start with him. He seems very shy, but I did catch him smiling at me and checking out my ass, so that's a plus. Holly told me he is a single dad with two boys. Skylar who is six and Mason who is nine.

I followed Holly back up toward the front by the register. Shelves hung on the wall lined with t-shirts, hats, shot glasses, beer mugs, bumper stickers, and other knick-knacks with KC's Bar & Grille printed on them. "What size t-shirt do you wear?" she asked.

"Medium," I replied. She handed me ten low-cut, V-neck t-shirts; five purple and five black, the bar colors. I notice that they are all smalls. "Wait, Holly, these are all small. I need medium. These will be too tight, my girls will be on display." I giggle and start to hand them back to her.

"KC believes that the more we look like Hooters girls, the more customers he will have." She rolls her eyes. "You should have seen the fight I had with him when he tried to make the uniform exactly like theirs. Be happy that it's just a tight t-shirt."

I really hope I get along with my new boss once I meet him. I said my goodbyes to everyone and told Holly I would see her at 11 AM.

AFTER I get home, I sit out back with a glass of wine and look up at the stars. It is a beautiful clear night. The longer I sit here, the more I think about Kyle. I miss him. I almost wish he was still around. I don't know if it would have changed anything I felt back then, but I should have confronted him. I should have grabbed that bitch by the hair and dragged her out of his bed. She had been trying for years to break us up. I just never expected it to work.

Even if I could forgive Kyle, he doesn't want me. He found out three years ago where I was. My grandma said that we belonged together and she wasn't keeping it from him any longer. But, I never heard from him. I waited two years after she told me he knew where I was, and nothing. I gave up and started seeing Daniel.

So many good memories had been made in this back yard. We used to sit together for hours planning our future. The first time he kissed me was out here. I have to stop thinking about him like this. It's time to face the fact that I am never going to see Kyle Connor again. It's time to move on; to stop thinking about the past and a future that would never be. I went inside, cleaned up the kitchen, showered, and went to bed hoping I wouldn't dream about him, too.

CHAPTER
Three

Amber

THREE WEEKS flew by and I found that I really enjoyed working at KC's. Holly and I became quick friends. She was the type of person that called it like she saw it. No sugar coating and definitely no filter. I like that about her, you don't have to wonder where she stands. I am a little softer spoken, so it is nice to have someone like her around; she tends to give me a little more self-confidence. We have had a few girls' nights with chick flicks, pizza, and lots of wine. It really is great to have a girlfriend to hang out with. I haven't had one since high school and never realized how much I missed it until now. Holly thinks I need to get back on the horse, so to speak, and find a man even if it is just casual. Sometimes I think that would be perfect for me, but I'm not sure I would be able to have that kind of relationship. There is a first time for everything, though, right?

It's Saturday night and apparently KC will be back. I am a little nervous to meet my boss for the first time. Though I'm not sure why, it has really been bothering me the last few days. Something about the whole atmosphere of the bar is so familiar, but not. Maybe it's just the fact that I used to work here when I was younger. I dressed a little differently than normal tonight and didn't even realize I was doing it at first. I usually wear my hair up, very little make-up, and jeans. Today, I took extra care in doing my hair and left it down and straightened my natural waves. I spent too long applying my make-up, giving my brown eyes a smoky look and my lips a light gloss. I put on my too-tight, purple KC's t-shirt with a pair of jean, cut-off shorts. They weren't obscene, but not something I would normally wear. My favorite pair of black cowboy boots topped off my outfit. I used to always wear those boots for Kyle. They were his favorite pair. I shook my head at the thought and finished getting ready. I looked pretty good; I was impressed with my reflection in the mirror. Hopefully I looked good enough that my new boss wouldn't fire me.

I walk into the bar and I swear it feels like everyone is staring at me. This is why I don't dress like this. I hate the attention. Holly lets out a whistle? "Look at you, sexy girl. I knew you had it in you!"

I roll my eyes at her. "Please, I just don't want to get fired the first time I meet KC for not living up to his Hooter-ific standards." I laugh.

"Well, you look hot. Keep that up and you are going to have every guy in town trying to get with you. And, Amber, that's not a bad thing," she says, raising her eyebrow.

"Says the girl who already has a great man," I scoff at her.

"Ha! True. Hey, could you help out the boys in the kitchen for a little bit? They have a large to-go order to put together and could use a hand finishing."

"Sure, no problem." I smile and head to the back room to put my purse away. I am in the kitchen, finishing up the last of the food for the to-go order, when Holly comes in and says that KC and the boys are here. She drags me out to meet them.

"Amber, this is Paul Walters." I shake his hand. Holly is one lucky woman. This man is gorgeous. He is close to a foot taller than me at six-foot-two with shoulder-length blond hair and beautiful green eyes. He has an amazing body, slim with just the right amount of muscles, especially in his arms, but I guess that goes with the territory of being a drummer.

"It's nice to meet you, Paul. Holly has told me a lot about you." He smiles.

"Uh oh, I swear I didn't do half of what she says." He laughs while trying to dodge a punch in the arm from Holly.

I can see by the way they look at each other how in love they are.

I am happy for her. From what I could tell in the short time I have known her, it seems like she has had a rough life. I am also a little jealous, though. I wish I had someone to look at me the way Paul looks at Holly.

Next, I met Marcus Winters, the bass player. He's shorter, five-foot-seven, with a shaved head and pewter gray eyes. Again, he has an amazing body. Where did these guys come from? We talk for a couple minutes and he tells me about his wife, Taryn, and their four year old son, Chase. His love for them is obvious from the sparkle in his eyes as he talks about them. It is really sweet and he seems really nice. Again, I feel that little bit of nagging jealousy.

Then, there is Angel Walker, the lead guitarist. All I can say is *holy fuck*. I know why his mama named him Angel. He's about six-foot of all hard muscle, short, spiky, chocolate brown hair, and eyes that are an amazing cyan. He kisses the back of my hand and says what a pleasure it is to meet me. Oh yeah, he is smooth. I bet he has girls dropping their panties with a smile. And, I'm probably drooling and staring like an idiot. Oh well, I'm sure he's used to it.

Holly comes up behind me, grabs my shoulders, and turns me around. "Amber this is our boss, Kyle Connor, or KC." As soon as the words leave her mouth, I feel all of the blood drain from my body and I tremble. It couldn't be! In the three weeks of working here, how could I not have realized this? How did I not know this was his bar? How did I not know he lived here in town? How had I not put it together? I had been wanting to see him again, right? I thought so, but maybe not so much.

At least I am not the only one that is completely floored. He looks just as shocked.

"What the fuck is she doing here?" Kyle growls at Holly. I can't move. Why is he so angry? That isn't a response I would have imagined from him. I didn't do anything wrong. Hell, he cheated on me! I should be angry, not him. Although, maybe I shouldn't have left without a word. Still, he fucked up first! It is taking everything I have to hold back the tears threatening to spill from my eyes. I refuse to cry! Especially right now.

"Do you two know each other?" Holly looks between the two of us like she is watching a tennis match. Finally, I snap out of it. All of a sudden, that anger I felt the day I caught him cheating, comes back to me.

"Oh, you could say that. Remember the asshole I was telling you about from high school, Holly? The one who cheated on me? Well this is that asshole." I never took my eyes off of Kyle. He is fuming. His cobalt eyes fix on me and I don't think he blinks them once. His hands are at his sides, fists clenching. He shakes his head and looks at me, confused. Then, he grabs my arm and drags me into the back to his office.

He pushes me through the door and closes it behind him. We stand there for what seems like hours, just staring at each other. If it is possible, he is even better looking than he was six years ago. He was still a boy then, but he is all man now. Just looking at him has butterflies dancing in my stomach and my heart beating double-time. He's six-foot-three with dark brown hair that's not too long, but not too short. It is perfect for running your fingers through or grabbing a hold of when ... I better not go there right now. His facial hair is sexy as hell, not too much, just like he hasn't shaved in a couple of days. And his body ... is amazing. He has definitely been hitting the gym. Through his tight, white t-shirt you can tell his arms and chest are muscular in all the right places with one very impressive set of abs. He has on a pair of loose-fitting jeans that hang off his hips just right, but let you see that he has a spectacular ass. And, of course, he has his signature, brown cowboy boots on. They are actually the boots I bought him for his eighteenth birthday. When I look back to his face for just a quick second, the anger is gone. He seems amused that I am checking him out ... but that is oh so brief.

"What are you doing here, Amber? And why are you working in my bar?" he asks, trying to sound angry, but there is a quiver in his voice that makes me think he is a little nervous.

Wow, I guess this isn't going to be a happy reunion.

"I moved back to town a little over a month ago. And, when I got a job here, I didn't know this was your bar. Hell, I didn't even know you still lived here. Last I knew, you lived in L.A."

He shakes his head. The angry fire coming back into his eyes.

"So, if you knew I lived here, you wouldn't have come back?" he spits. Okay, now I am getting pissed. He cheated on me, not the other way around. What in the hell is he so pissed off about?

"That is *not* what I said. I don't know what your problem is with me, exactly, but if anyone should be angry, it should be me. You are the one who cheated—"

"That is the second time you said that ... I *never* cheated on you! I am pissed because you left one day without saying a word. No reason, no goodbye, nothing. Hell, it took me three fucking years to find out where you went!" He interrupts, throwing his hands up in the air. Before he puts his head down, I can see sadness in his eyes. Then, it hits me. Holly said he was in love and the girl took off without saying goodbye. Was that me?

"Kyle, I left town because I was heartbroken. I went to surprise you with tickets I had won and found Nora in your bed ... naked." The last part comes out as a whisper, the fire dying in my voice. It still hurts to think about it, but hurts so much worse to say it out loud.

He looks pissed again. "Fuck! I can't believe you would think for a second that I would do that to you! And with her, of all people! I came out of the shower and found her in my bed. I was pissed. I guess she thought if I saw what she had to offer, I wouldn't be able to resist. She was sadly mistaken. I told her to get her ass dressed and get out. I found those tickets in the envelope by the front door but never knew where they came from. After I got rid of Nora, I went to your house to tell you what she pulled and show you the tickets, but your grandparents said you were sick. You wouldn't answer your phone or texts. I came back after two days and you were gone." He leans on the corner of his desk. "Do you have any idea what kinds of things went through my head? I thought maybe I did something wrong, but for the life of me I couldn't figure out what it was. Then, I started thinking maybe it was all a lie. Maybe you never really loved me. You didn't have the guts to tell me to my face, so you just took off without a word. No matter what scenario I came up with in my head for why you left, it didn't change the one main thing..." He stands from his desk and walks over to me until we are almost touching chest to chest. He waits until I look up at him before he finishes what he is saying. "You ripped my fucking heart to shreds the day you left." You could almost feel the pain dripping from each word.

It felt like someone shot a dagger into my heart. I don't know what to say to him. Nothing I say can make it better. I screwed up by running. He didn't do anything. I could see it in his eyes that he was telling the truth. It was all my fault. All this time he thought I just up and left him. And I was too stupid to get an explanation for what I saw. I just believed he would betray me, let my own insecurities fuel my emotions. I understand why he was so angry when he saw me. I would have been, too. I don't blame him for hating me. Hell, right now I hate myself. I wish I would have talked to him back then and let him explain.

"You know me better than anyone. Even now, after six years, I bet you still know me better than anyone else. You know what kind of person I am. How much I despise people who cheat. I would never do that, especially to you. Deep down, you know that."

"I get it. I would be pissed at me, too. I was just so hurt, I wasn't thinking clearly. I'm so sorry." I try to hold back the tears, but I am doing a lousy job. Tears start to flow and I can't stop them. "Look, Kyle, I'm going to go home for the night. Think over what you want to do. I understand if you don't want me working here. Just have Holly call me when you have an answer." I turn toward the door and stop without looking back to him. "I'm sorry. I know you hate me and I don't blame you. I loved you so much. The thought of you with someone else crushed me and I just reacted. I couldn't think past the pain." Before he could say anything, I run out of the office, grab my purse, and leave through the kitchen.

CHAPTER
Four

Kyle

I AM THE biggest fucking asshole. I just stood here and watched her leave. I have been waiting for six years to be near her again. When I finally am, I let her walk away. My head is so fucked up right now, if I don't think this through a little first I could end up making it a lot worse. God, when she turned around it was like a bolt of lightning hit me. She is so beautiful, still so fucking beautiful. It's hard to breathe when she looks at me. Her hair is longer than it used to be, but it's still that perfect shade of caramel brown. Her body hasn't changed a bit, the same perfect curves in all the right places. She still makes me hard the instant I lay eyes on her. She is the only woman that has ever had that effect on me. I should have just locked her in my office and fucked her on my desk until we both remembered how good we were together. But, I don't think she would have responded well to that, especially after the way she high-tailed it out of here. All this time she thought I cheated on her with that skank Nora. I can't believe she didn't trust me. I was going to propose to her, why would I cheat on her? Duh, dipshit, she didn't know that.

I am so pissed at myself, at Nora, at Amber. I grab the beer bottle from my desk, tip it back, empty it, and then chuck the bottle at my door. I lean back in my chair and close my eyes. How in the hell am I going to fix this mess? I still love her. I never stopped loving her, but seeing her, the sparks I felt when I grabbed her and pulled her in here, just proves even more what I already know.

"Glad I didn't open the door a few seconds earlier." I lift my head up to see Paul closing the door behind him, making himself at home in the chair at the other end of my desk. I met Paul in L.A. We have been best friends ever since. He has had the pleasure of hearing my bitch ass drone on about Amber since the day we met.

"So, how did it go in here? We saw her tear out of the parking lot and Holly is a little worried. Did you find out why she up and left before?"

"Oh, I found out all right. It was all over a stupid fucking misunderstanding brought on by a skanky bitch. It could have all been avoided if she would have just talked to me before she left." Paul is quiet for a minute after I finish. I can tell he is processing both sides before he speaks. He is great when you need advice. He won't tell you what he thinks you want to hear. He tells you what he thinks and even though I don't always like it, he's usually right.

"Do you still love her?" he asks, even though he already knows my answer.

"Yes, I do. I wasn't really sure before, but I was the second I saw her again."

"Think about this then, what if you walked in her house and saw what she saw? Some dude naked in her bed? Would you really want to face her to hear some bullshit apology or excuse that would surely follow? Plus, she was only eighteen. Hard to handle something maturely when you aren't really mature yet."

"No way. I wouldn't have just left the state without talking to her, or at least beating the shit out of the guy."

"What about the time you went to find her in Atlanta and left without talking to her?"

"That was different. The guy was proposing to her. She said yes. She looked happy. Oh God, I never thought about him. What if they got married? Is he here with her?"

"Relax, dude, that's why she came back. Holly said she never married him. She came home and found him in bed with another chick. So, she left his sorry ass and came back here."

"So, all I have to do is figure out how to get her to fall in love with me again." Maybe I would get lucky and she had never stopped loving me. One could hope.

"Good luck with that. Right now, though, we have some music to play." With a slap on the shoulder, we headed out to play our set.

Being on stage, playing music, always relaxes me and helps me clear my head for a while. While I was in L.A., I realized really fast that I didn't want the life of a famous rock star. I never really did. After I met Paul and we formed Bleeding Hearts, we found Marcus and Angel. We played around L.A. for three years and were starting to get pretty well-known. Even that early on. I didn't like who I was becoming. The other guys felt the same way. I wanted to come back to Oakville and the guys came with me. My dream was always a place like KC's. Amber and I used to talk about opening a place like it all the time. I'm surprised Amber never realized this place was mine. The most obvious hint is the name being my initials. The color scheme for the place are her favorite colors, purple and black. Amber worked here back when the place was The Shack. Our first date was here. Shit, the booth that has "Kyle luvs Amber" carved into it is still in the back corner. I was thrilled when I came back and saw it up for sale. I bought the place a week later and started the renovations.

It was then that I decided I needed to find her and get her back. Even though I had no idea as to why she left, I didn't care. I was willing to fight for her. I went to see Amber's grandmother and begged for her to tell me where she was. She told me that she believed we belonged together. She thought we had already been apart for too long and gave me her address. Two days before I was supposed to leave, we found out my mom had breast cancer. My trip was put on hold until my mom was healthy again. I was afraid to leave her, plus, I just opened the bar. Then, my father passed away. By the time it seemed right to go to find Amber, two more damn years had gone by. A little over a year ago, I finally got in my car and headed to Atlanta. I had to do something. She may not want me, but I could finally stop wondering. At the very least, I would have the chance to ask her why she left in the first place. I had a million scenarios in my head for how this trip could play out. What actually happened wasn't even on my radar.

I knocked on her apartment door, but no one answered. I decided to go to the coffee shop across the street and wait a while. I sat by the window. I could see her if she came home from here. I was so damn nervous I didn't know if she was going to slap me or hug me when she

*saw me. I was really hoping for the latter. But, it didn't matter. I couldn't
live without her anymore and I was going to prove that I wasn't going
anywhere. I have never loved anyone the way I loved her. I never would.
If I didn't have her, I would spend the rest of my life alone.*

*Just like that, there she was, more beautiful than ever. My smile
quickly faded when I saw that some douche-looking guy was with her.
They were holding hands. He stopped her right in front of the window
of the coffee shop. Then, Mr. Douche got down on one knee and pulled
a black box from his pocket. Really? Who proposes on the street in front
of a coffee shop? I wanted her to say no so badly, I didn't realize I was
holding my breath. I could see the look on her face. She's shocked, but
happy. He opened the box and pulled the ring out and slipped it on her
finger. As if my world hadn't been turned upside down enough in the last
few years, I saw her nod her head in agreement. I watched them walk
across to her apartment building and go inside. I got up and left, driving
straight back home and head first into the bottle. I didn't come up for air
for three weeks.*

We finish our last song, I head over to the bar for a beer with the
guys, and then head back to my apartment for the night. As soon as I
walk in, I know someone is here. My heart stars to race in my chest. Was
it Amber? Did she come back to talk to me? Does she still want me? I
pick up my pace, walking faster to my room. I push open the door and
see Darcie. FUCK! I have been trying to get rid of this woman for over
a year now. She is not taking the fucking hint. I met Darcie in the bar
after I got back from Atlanta, I was drunk all of the time and screwing a
different woman every night. I went home with her one night. We were
just about to finish up when her husband walked into the bedroom.
She never told me she was married. I may have been a whore, but I had
morals. I never messed around with someone else's girl. To top it off,
her husband just happened to be Beau Hartly. He and I never got along
in high school. That night ended with both of us in jail.

"What are you doing in my apartment?"

"It's been so long, Kyle. I know you miss me. Come on, I can make
you feel *very* good." She thinks she sounds sexy, but she doesn't. A year
of pulling shit like this and not giving up just makes her desperate.
She knows what kind of guy I am, no woman more than once and
definitely no relationships.

"Look, Darcie, I'm starting to sound like a fucking broken record.
I do not want you. That is not going to change, *ever*. If I find you in my

apartment again, I will have you arrested. Now, get out." I try to keep my voice even, calm. The last thing I want is to set her off.

"I would never walk out on you like that bitch Amber did." How did she know about Amber? I'm sure Beau has seen her since she started working at the bar. He always did have a thing for her.

"You are pushing your luck, Darcie. I suggest you shut the fuck up."

"You really think once little miss goody two shoes finds out how many women you have been with she is going to want anything to do with you? You'll be back in my bed again." She smirked and out she went. I lock up behind her and make a mental note to change the locks. I am starting to think she is the kind of bitch that boils bunnies.

I turn the shower on as hot as I can stand it. I relax under the spray of the water and close my eyes. The only thing going through my mind is Amber ... how good she looked with a tight KC's t-shirt and her ass in those short jean shorts. I place my hand above my head on the wall, rest my forehead on the cool tile, and start to stroke myself. Just thinking about how she looked got me hard. I want to touch her, though; it has been too long since I have had her warm and naked beneath me as I am kissing every inch of her soft curvy skin. God, I have to get her back, if I get this worked up thinking about her, it is going to be so amazing to actually feel her again.

CHAPTER
Five

Amber

I PARK MY car in the driveway and slowly get out. I am so stupid. I could have saved us both a lot of heartache and tears if I would have just talked to him instead of running away like a child. No wonder he hates me. How could he not? I bypass the wine, grab a bottle of tequila and a shot glass, and flop down on a stool at the island. I fill the small glass and tip it back, letting the alcohol burn down the back of my throat.

He's right. I didn't trust him. I knew in my heart he would never hurt me, that he loved me, but the second that I saw something that made me question it, I bolted instead of giving him a chance. I tip back another shot, hopefully after a few more of these I will be too numb to think about it. I should have known better. He would have never touched Nora. I knew he hated her as much as I did. She should have been my first sign that something was off. Shot number three … starting to feel better now. I grab the tequila and make my way outside.

I sit in the chair by the fire pit and take another drink. The tears start and they won't stop.

Kyle's hand is running along my cheek and tracing my lips. "Amber, wake up," he whispers, his voice deep and sexy. "Mmm," I reply, feeling goose bumps rise on my skin as his hot breath grazes my neck. I wait for the kiss, for his tongue to run across my skin. I can feel myself become needy, waiting, anticipating his next move. Instead, his voice gets louder, "Wake up, Amber!"

I jump out of the chair and quickly realize this is not a dream. He is standing right in front of me. "Jesus, Kyle, you scared the shit out of me! What are you doing here? What time is it?" The tequila is still in full effect because I am spinning, and damn, if I thought seeing one Kyle was hot and sexy, seeing two is even hotter. I giggle at the thought of two Kyles and continue to check him out. Of course he sees this. He is looking at me with a raised eyebrow, that sexy smirk of his playing on his lips.

"Easy, Princess, one question at a time."

I stumble back down into the chair. I haven't been called that in so long; it was what he always called me. What is he doing here? Did he come here to yell at me some more for being so damn stupid? God, I hope not. There's only so much my heart can take within twenty-four hours.

"I'm sorry I scared you. I was trying not to, but you were out cold. I can see why." He picks up the bottle of tequila and shakes it ... I try to grab it from him, but it is no use seeing as he towers over me. "I don't think you need any more of this tonight." He looks at his watch. "It's three in the morning. I'm here because I needed to see you. I was a dick earlier." He looks down at the ground and runs his fingers through his hair. "I never should have let you leave earlier. Can we go inside? Have some coffee and talk?" All I can do is nod. If I try to talk, I am going to sound like a blubbering idiot.

Kyle follows me into the house. He puts the cap on the tequila and puts it away while I start a pot of coffee. "Wow, the kitchen looks great. I heard that you did some remodeling a while back," he says, that killer smile planted on his lips.

"I think I always knew I would be back here someday and this place only needed a few touch-ups to make it perfect."

"I know how much you love this house and what it means to you. I am really sorry about your grandparents, you know how much I cared about them. They were the closest thing I ever had to grandparents growing up."

"They loved you, too. You know that, right? I was the reason they wouldn't tell you where I was. I asked them not to. But, I never told them why. I didn't want them to have a reason to hate you. I knew how important they were to you." He places his hand on mine and slowly moves his thumb back and forth over the top of my wrist. Butterflies invade my stomach from his touch and the way he looks at me with those blue eyes. I could get lost in those beautiful blue eyes. The coffee pot beeps and I quickly get up. I pour out two mugs and bring them to the island where he is already prepared with milk and sugar. We sit on the couch. He sits so close to me, barely touching, that I find it hard to breathe. I let out a shaky breath, and breathe in deeply. I can smell his cologne. Eternity. I bought it for him for Valentine's Day when we were in tenth grade.

"It was always your favorite. I have been wearing it since I was fifteen." Shit, now I get busted smelling him? I need to change the subject. My body is alert and on fire. Having him so close... I take a gulp of coffee hoping it will clear my tequila fog. I'm so close to throwing caution to the wind and saying, "Screw it!" It takes everything in me to not straddle his hips. With the way he is looking at me, I don't think he would put up a fight.

"I know Gram told you where I lived three years ago. Why didn't you ever contact me?" The smirk is gone and he looks so sad. He tells me about the bar and his parents. "Kyle, I am so sorry you had to deal with all of that at once." He gives me a sad smile and nods, taking a big breath.

"About a year ago, just before your grandparents passed away, I did go to get you back. You weren't home, so I waited in the coffee shop across the street." He laughs, but it isn't a happy one. "It was just my luck that I pick the same day some douchey guy decides to propose to you right in front of me."

Oh my God! What are the chances? I cannot believe he was there that day. So close to me and I never knew it. "If I would have known you were there, I never would have said yes."

He grabs my hand and holds it, but I continue before he can say anything. "I didn't date anyone. Four years after I left and I still couldn't find it in me to date. I was a mess. I met Daniel right after I got to Atlanta. I told him it would be a long time before I was in any shape to move on from you. He said he was happy to be my friend. And, a good friend he was. At a time when I really needed one, there he was. I never should have dated him. I definitely shouldn't have agreed to marry him. I loved him like a friend … not like I love you." Oh, shit! Did I just say that out loud? Maybe he didn't catch that. His head snaps up. Shit…he caught it.

"Did you say love?"

"Of course. I will always love you."

"Enough to be with me again?" he asks, sounding hopeful.

"I thought you were angry? That you hated me for what I did?" My voice breaks up a lot more than I want it to. Kyle grabs my face in his hands and pulls me toward him. We are so close, I can feel his breath on my lips.

"I could never hate you. You are the only woman I have ever loved… will ever love. I was angry for a long time. I had no idea why you left. Actually, I was hurt more than anything. But, you know me, anger is easier to deal with."

"I want nothing more than to be with you again, but I don't think jumping in head first is the way to do it. We have missed out on six years of each other's lives. We need to get to know each other again." I search his face, trying to see what he is thinking. His expression is one that I can't quite read.

"I can agree to that for a little while, Princess," he says. He moves his lips against my ear and whispers, "We are going to have to get to know each other again quickly, though. It is killing me to be around you and not have all of you." A shiver runs down my spine. He definitely wasn't like this before. This new aggressive side of him may be my undoing. "It's really late. I am going to stay here with you and fall asleep holding you in my arms. Do you have any objections to that?" He gives me a look that dares me to challenge him. The only problem I have is whether or not I am able to keep my hands to myself with him that close to me.

"As long as that's all there is, I have no objections."

We lock all the doors, turn out the lights, and head upstairs. I give him a toothbrush and head to find something to wear. After he finishes in the bathroom, I go in to get ready for bed.

When I come out he is on the edge of the bed in a pair of black silk boxers. My mouth waters and my knees start to buckle. This is going to be absolute torture. Seeing every line of every hard muscle on his body, feeling him lying next to me almost naked, I'm going to need a really big douse of self-control. Judging by the smile on his face, he knows damn well what he is doing to me. That's okay; two can play this game.

Instead of walking around the bed, I crawl over his legs, making sure my ass is in full view in my too-short sleep shorts. As I cross over him, I can tell I accomplished what I set out to do from the groan he lets out before flopping down on his back and squeezing his eyes closed. I roll onto my side with a smile and flip the lamp off. I feel him ease up behind me. He snakes one arm under my neck, the other around my waist, and he pulls me in as close as he can. I gasp when I feel his erection against my ass.

"I told you, Princess. Just knowing you're here, makes me hard. You don't play fair," he whispers in my ear. I don't say a word. I just wiggle my backside into him a little more. I am rewarded with another groan and a firm grip on my hip. "I will be breaking our deal if you keep that up," he growls. I am so tempted to just give us both what we want, but I can't. I just…can't. "G'night, Princess … I've missed you."

"Good night, Kyle. I've missed you, too." I entwine his fingers with mine and kiss the back of his hand as I drift off to sleep.

CHAPTER
Six

Kyle

$\mathcal{I}$ HAVE BEEN laying here awake for the last two hours. I don't want to open my eyes. I haven't felt this relaxed and peaceful since before she left. This morning, waking up with Amber in my arms, is a dream come true. I don't ever want it to end. Her head is resting on my chest and I can feel her warm breath every time she exhales. Her smooth leg is wrapped around my thigh. Her arm is so tight around my waist it's as if she's holding me in place. I lean my head down just enough to rest my nose in her hair and inhale. God, she smells so good. She uses the same coconut scented shampoo she always did. I breathe her in again. I love that smell. Apparently, so does my cock. It starts twitching, coming to life. I am not a horny, hormonal, teenager anymore, but being around her still makes me feel like one.

I understand what she meant last night about getting to know each other again, but I am terrified of what she is going to think of me after she finds out about all the alcohol, drugs, and women. I am not making excuses, but I was in a bad place trying to forget her any way I could. I am not proud of everything I did, but when it came to the women I was with, I was always up front. They knew before anything happened that I only wanted a physical encounter, no emotions involved. It may make me sound like a dick, but hey, I was honest. At least I didn't lead anyone on, thinking I was going to fall in love. I knew that was never going to happen, so there was no use pretending. There have been a few that thought they possessed something special and would be the one to change my mind. I quickly set them straight. The only one that hasn't seem to have gotten the memo is Darcie. She can be a sneaky, heartless bitch when she wants something. The last time a girl like her came around, Amber left, and I will be damned if that is going to happen again. I am going to have to make Amber see that she is the only woman I want. For us to work, we are going to have to be totally honest with each other. I just hope she can accept my past and leave it behind us. I guess now is as good a time as any to start our talk, even though the thought has my stomach turning.

I lightly kiss the top of her head. I begin to trail my finger from her shoulder slowly down her arm, then along her ribs to her hip, leaving goose bumps in its wake. I continue over her stomach around her navel, then I trace slowly up between her breasts. She gasps and opens her eyes to look at me. I bring my finger along her jaw, trace her lips, and slowly bring my face closer to hers. I can see her chest begin to rise and fall more quickly the closer I get. Her tongue peeks out to wet her lips. She wants me to kiss her. I wasn't planning on it, I don't want to push, but there was no denying that's what she wants right now. Who was I to deny my Princess something she clearly wanted? Yes, I am a selfish bastard; I admit it. But, there is something about this woman that makes me lose any self-control I have. I slowly bring my lips to hers and whisper, "Good," then kiss her softly, "Morning," kiss her softly again, "Princess." The last time I press a little harder against her lips.

"Mmmmm." She starts running her fingers through my hair. I can't hold back. I suck at her lips, teasing them apart. When she opens them, I thrust my tongue in her mouth, ready to taste her. She feels just like I remember. So sweet. I pull her closer to me and my erection rubs against her inner thigh. She lets out the sexiest groan I have ever heard and I almost embarrass myself right there in my boxers. I do not want to stop this, but I have to. I can't go any further until she knows everything and still wants me, despite. Plus, I made a promise last night to go slow. I intend to keep it until she decides otherwise. I cup her cheeks in my hands and slowly pull away.

"As much as I don't want to ... we need to stop, Princess. We have a lot of things to talk about."

"I know. Can I just say wow? You have gotten a lot better at that, and it was pretty amazing before." She gives me a little wink. I smile, but inside I am worried that when she finds out how I got so much better, she won't feel the same.

"Okay, Princess, how about you take a shower and get dressed. I will go down and fix us some breakfast." She looks a little shocked.

"You can cook? We are talking more than Lucky Charms, right?" She giggles and pokes me in the ribs. I have to get out of this bed before I lose all self-control.

"Yes, I can cook, a lot more than cereal. I do own a restaurant, remember? I took a few cooking classes over the last few years just in case I needed them." Before that beautiful smile could do me in, I hop out of bed and start putting on my jeans. "Shower, Princess, then meet me in the kitchen." I kiss her forehead and walk out the bedroom door.

Amber

WATCHING HIM pull up and button those jeans hanging low on his hips is doing nothing to calm my desire for him. The only thing sexier than a man in nothing but a pair of jeans is Kyle Connor in nothing but a pair of jeans. When he turns and struts out the door, I can't help but want to reach out and run my hand all over his perfect ass. I am glad one of us has will power. I never would have been able to stop. I haven't slept that well since the last time I spent the night in his arms. I've been awake for hours, but I didn't want to end the bliss of being wrapped in his arms. I know I said we need to take this slow, but I am not sure I can. Most of the time, he seems like the same Kyle, like nothing has changed. Other times, I see that the man he has become is so different than the boy he was. He is cocky, confident, and sexy; a strong man who will take charge and isn't afraid to tell you exactly what he wants and when. And, I love it. This dominant side of him sends tingles straight to my core.

He has also seemed to master making women want him. Holly told me a few weeks ago that he hasn't stayed with anyone for more than a night or two. How many women has he been with in the last six years?

I guess I need to decide if I am going to let that bother me. I honestly think it would bother me more if he was in a serious relationship and had actually loved someone else.

I finally make it into the shower. I close my eyes and can't help but visualize Kyle with all kinds of different women. My insides twist into knots, but I can't punish him for it. I am the one who left without a word. I finish in the shower, towel dry my hair, and put it in a high ponytail. I quickly get dressed in just some jean shorts and a plain white t-shirt. I can already smell coffee and breakfast cooking downstairs, and my mouth is watering.

As I come down the stairs, I hear music playing and Kyle's sexy, deep voice singing along in the kitchen. I peek around the corner and it takes everything in me to control myself when I see the image before me. Remember when I said there is nothing sexier than Kyle Connor in nothing but jeans? Well, I was so very wrong. I lean against the doorway to the kitchen to take in the sight in front of me. How I keep from becoming a puddle on the floor, I do not know. Kyle faces the stove, cooking French toast with his bare muscular back on display. On his right shoulder blade is the tattoo he got for his seventeenth birthday. It is the logo for the band Breaking Benjamin. He has some new ones on his arm, too. One is a black guitar with angel wings and another on his chest over his heart that I assume is his band's logo. The tattoo is a heart with angel wings, cracked up the center with drops of blood in the shapes of tear drops dripping from the bottom. There is something written in the corner, but I couldn't see it that well last night.

The song changes and he starts singing along again, his hips swaying back and forth with the beat. All I can think about is what those hips could do with me lying underneath him. Suddenly, it's starting to get very hot in this kitchen.

"You enjoying the show, Princess?" He looks over his shoulder and winks before going back to cooking. How did he know I was there? I definitely hit the nail on the head about him being cocky and confident. The last thing I am going to do is stroke his ego.

"Eh ... kind of." I shrug my shoulders and head for the coffee pot. Before I can register what's happening, Kyle has picked me up and placed me on top of the counter. He moves closer, placing himself between my legs. He runs his hands along my bare thighs. He moves up higher and higher with each pass until his rough fingers are grazing the edges of my lace panties. He brings his lips to my ear." Don't lie, Princess. I know when you're turned on. I can see it in your eyes. I can hear you breathing harder over the music, and right now..." He slips his finger inside my panties and runs it along my folds down to my entrance, just enough to feel how turned on I really am. He slowly moves his finger back and forth, just enough to tease. I can't hold back the whimper.

"I can feel how wet you are for me. I would say you thought my show was more than just okay. Care to retract your statement?" He lightly nips my earlobe with his teeth.

"Depends. What will happen if I don't?" I can feel him smile against my cheek. "Oh God." He pushes two fingers inside of me, teasing them in and out slowly, while circling my clit with his thumb. My entire body feels like it is on fire. He trails his tongue up my neck, and when he gets back to my ear, he whispers "Feels good, huh?" All I can do is nod and whimper. How this man could have me ready to explode in seconds is beyond me. He chuckles softly.

"How about now, have you changed your mind yet?" He starts moving his fingers faster and harder now.

"A... almost," is all I can say. Judging by the smile on his face, he knows I am not talking about changing my mind, but instead the orgasm that was about to rip through me.

"Look at me, Amber. I want to watch your beautiful face when you come." I look at him and can feel the heat rush to my cheeks. This is definitely the side of Kyle I am not familiar with, but I am really liking it. Before I know it, I am crying out his name, my entire body shuddering.

"Fucking beautiful." He buries his face in my neck, placing soft kisses on my skin. "Did that change your mind?" he asks against my neck.

"If that's what happens when I disagree with you, don't count on me being very agreeable." He kisses my forehead.

"You don't have to disagree with me ... I will make you come whenever and wherever you want. All you have to do is ask." This man is going to kill me. I kiss his chest and notice what's in the corner of his tattoo. It is my name. I am a little surprised by this.

"Can I ask you something?"

"Anything, babe," he answers.

"Why do you have my name on your tattoo?" He turns to face me.

"Because you are my heart. When you left, my heart was broken." He gives me a sad smile, fixes my shorts, washes up, and goes back to fixing breakfast.

At this, I can't help the twinge of guilt I feel in my chest.

Kyle

I AM sitting out in the backyard waiting for Amber to finish cleaning the breakfast mess, which she insisted on doing since I cooked. I probably went a little too far in the kitchen earlier, but I couldn't help it. She looked too damn cute standing there all hot and bothered, watching me in the kitchen. Besides, she didn't seem to mind one single bit. Just hearing her sexy little noises and watching her face as I got her off ... damn, I almost lost it, and she never even had to touch me.

Luckily, she walks outside before I can get all excited thinking about her again. She sits down next to me on the double lounger and hands me a glass of iced tea. "I thought you might need something to cool you down." She has no idea, or maybe she does by the way she smiles at me.

"So, do who starts talking first?" she asks.

It might as well be me. I have a feeling there isn't anything she has done over the last six years that would cause us any problems. I run my hands down my face then grab her hand. Here goes nothing. "I waited here the first six months, hoping you would come back or call. The more time that passed, the angrier I got. I just didn't understand. One day, we're planning out our lives together, and the next, you disappear. I started thinking maybe you didn't love me as much as I loved you ... or even at all.

"I decided that I needed to get as far away from this place as possible. Everything reminded me of you. So, I packed up my car and headed to L.A. I met Paul in a club one night after I got so shitfaced I couldn't stand up straight. He helped me out of the club, found out I was living in my car, and offered me his couch to crash on. He got me a job waiting tables at a club he was tending bar at. We became friends pretty quickly and decided to put a band together. We eventually found Marcus and Angel and started Bleeding Hearts." I look up at her to make sure she is still with me. She gives me an encouraging smile, so I continue.

"I came up with the name. I thought it was poetic at the time. We started playing clubs and getting a little more well-known. But, my mind was still on you. So, I did anything I could to make myself forget, if only for a little while. I started drinking way too much and using drugs on occasion. Luckily, the drugs never got serious. When the drugs and alcohol weren't enough, I figured the company of the endless supply of women would do the trick." I give her a pleading look and gripped her hand tighter, praying she understands how sorry I am. God, I hope this isn't where she tells me to fuck off forever.

"I am going to be honest, Amber, there were a lot more women than I remember, but I was always careful and got tested frequently, I swear." I look into the yard. I can't find it in me to look at her face.

"Kyle, it's okay. It doesn't matter what you did while we were apart. As long as it is all over now and we are totally honest with each other about everything, it will be okay. Don't get me wrong, I am not saying I like thinking about you being with other women, but I can't hold things that you did when we weren't together against you. Especially since I was the reason we weren't together. I am so sorry for not having more faith in you. I am sorry for not having the guts to stick around and talk to you about what I saw. I hope you can forgive me for causing all of your pain."

"I have already forgiven you. I can't say I would have handled the situation any better if it were reversed. You know I'm a strong believer in the saying, "Everything happens for a reason." Maybe those six years apart were meant to show us just how much we really do mean to each other. You are the only woman I have ever loved. Now that I know what it is like without you in my life, I will do everything in my power to make sure that doesn't happen again." With that, I grab her face and kiss her with as much intensity as I can muster. I try to let all the love I feel for her show through this kiss. When we stop the kiss to catch our breath, I can see how much she loves me in her eyes.

"You are the only man I have ever truly loved. All these years, I have never stopped thinking about you and wishing I was with you. I am so happy that we have another chance. I promise, I won't screw this one up." I pull her close to me and just hold her in my arms. I finally feel whole again. My chest no longer feels like it is going to burst from the agonizing pain I was in. Now, it feels like it could burst from the overwhelming love and happiness.

CHAPTER
Seven

Kyle

THE PAST month has been great. I can't believe I have Amber back in my life. I had given up all hope that this would ever happen. Even though it is killing me and I have taken more cold showers in the last month than I have since I hit puberty, I am taking things slowly like she wanted to. I should get some kind of medal for being able to keep my hands to myself. Lying next to her all night, every night and not being buried deep inside her is about to kill me, but I am keeping my promise.

"Hey, man, what are ya up to?" Paul asks, walking into my office.

"Just some paper work. Is it getting busy out there?"

"It's getting there." If there is anyone who knew how screwed up I was after I lost Amber, it is Paul. He has stood by me through a lot of shit over the last six years. We have had each other's back no matter what.

"Looks like things have been going pretty well lately with you and Amber … I really like her, so does Holly." I smile because I can't help but smile at anything Amber related.

"Yeah things are going really good. I never thought I would have her back."

Paul looked down at his watch. "Let's go get a drink and say hi to our girls before we need to start our set."

"Sounds good." I clap him on the back and follow him out to the bar.

I have always liked Saturday nights here. It's the night Bleeding Hearts plays. It's even better now knowing Amber is here watching. I see her at the bar waiting on an order. I slip up behind her and touch my lips to her ear. I feel her shiver.

"Hey there, beautiful, can I buy you a drink?"

"I'm not sure my very sexy boyfriend would like that."

"You think I'm sexy?" I kiss behind her ear, down her neck, and back up to her ear.

She turns around, wraps her arms around my neck, and whispers in my ear, "So sexy that I have a hard time keeping my hands off you. And, I don't want to anymore. You play your cards right and tonight I will end our suffering." She gives me a kiss on the cheek, grabs her tray of drinks, and looks over her shoulder with a wink. I just shake my head and laugh. I am going to be hard all night now. Shit.

As if what Amber told me before I got on stage isn't distraction enough, I've been watching her sway those sexy ass hips to the music in a short, denim skirt with cowboy boots. As if on cue, she looks up at me and smiles. Little vixen. She knows damn well what she does to me. I have never wanted off this stage so badly in my whole life. We were great together six years ago, but it's different this time around. Everything seems stronger, more intense.

Paul nudges my shoulder and tilts his head to the door. Fuck, just what I need. Walking through the door are Beau Hartly and his buddies. Amber was friendly with him in high school and hung out with him a couple times, but there was never anything to it, as far as she was concerned. He thought they were dating. When we decided to become more than friends, he claimed that I stole her from him. Beau also blames me for his marriage falling apart. He and his wife obviously had problems to begin with or else she wouldn't have been picking up guys in bars, but that's beside the point. He hates me now. If I know Beau, he is going to cause as much shit as possible with Amber and me. I just hope she doesn't fall for his pretty-boy bullshit. And, of course he spots her right away and sits at one of her tables. Luckily, we only have one more song. Amber just spotted Beau and she doesn't look too happy to see him. I told her all about the shit with Darcie and Beau so she wouldn't end up blindsided by one of them.

As soon as we finish, I head straight to his table. "Beau ... haven't seen you in here for a while." By the shit-eating grin on his face, I know that he is here to make trouble. I look over my shoulder toward the bar. Luckily, Paul and the boys could sense it, too. They are ready and waiting.

"I heard Amber is back in town," he said as he glanced in her direction. Something flares inside of me. Driving my fist into his face suddenly sounds more than appealing. I don't want him anywhere near her. Just the sound of her name leaving his lips enrages me. "I thought I would come down here and see if there was still that old spark between us." I start to grab his sorry ass, but I feel Amber's hand on my back.

She whispers in my ear, "Calm down, baby ... I got this." She moves in front of me. "Beau, looks like things haven't changed much since I left. You two still can't get along." I don't like the way his slimy eyes are fixated on my girl.

"It's not easy to get along with a guy who first steals your girlfriend, then your wife." He gives me a smug smile like he just won a fucking prize.

"Well, I don't know about the wife part, but I was never your girlfriend, Beau, so he didn't steal me from you." He flinches, but ignores what she said.

"I came home one night after work to find Kyle in my bed fucking my wife." He thinks he's shocked her with this. She gives him a sympathetic look and shakes her head.

"Beau, sounds like you married quite the tramp. Now, if you boys would like a drink I will get ya one, but if you are just in here to make trouble, you can go. What will it be?" Beau stands up and glares at us both for a second, then storms out with his buddies trying to hide their laughter behind him. I look over at the bar. Paul, Angel, Marcus, and Holly are laughing their asses off.

"Princess, just when I thought there was no way you could turn me on any more, you go and put that asshole in his place." I wrap my arms around her waist and pull her close to my chest.

"What are the chances the boss will let us get out of here early tonight?" She smiles up at me.

"Why, Princess, what's the rush?" She pulls me down so she can whisper in my ear. "Because I need you to take me home, get me naked, and get inside me." She didn't need to say anything else. I picked her up over my shoulder as I walked by everyone at the bar.

"We are taking off a little early. See y'all later," I say, hearing their catcalls and laughter as I head out the door.

Amber

DURING THE ride from the bar to my house, we don't speak. Instead, we steal glances at each other. My pulse is racing, my hands are clammy, and there is a fluttering in my stomach. I don't know why I am nervous. It's not like we have never been together before. I lost my virginity to him for God's sake. It just seems like the anticipation is higher now than it was then. We pull up in my driveway. Kyle turns off the car. As soon as I close the door behind me, he scoops me up into his arms and kisses me as he walks us through the front door and up to my bedroom. He sets me down on the edge of the bed. "Don't move an inch, Princess, I will be right back." He places a chaste kiss on my lips and heads down stairs. A few minutes later, he returns with chilled champagne, glasses, and candles. It is perfect. He is perfect. I didn't know why I was waiting so long. It was killing me just as bad. But, this… this makes me happy I did. This man fills my heart to bursting. He makes me feel so loved and wanted and beautiful, with just a smoldering look. He places several candles around the room and pours us each a glass of champagne.

I watch him walk over to me. He's wearing nothing but his loose jeans, and I can't wait to get my hands all over him. He hands me my glass as I eye him appreciatively.

"To the most beautiful and amazing woman I have ever known. I am so lucky to have you back in my life." He touches his glass to mine and kisses me so softly, so sweetly, that it brings tears to my eyes. I take a drink, hoping to calm the overwhelming emotion.

"I think I am the lucky one. I love you so much. I promise I am going to do everything I can to make up for us missing out on the last six years together." He takes our glasses and sets them on the nightstand.

"I love you so much. You have nothing to apologize for, nor do you have anything to make up for. Like I said before, maybe there was a reason we were apart all that time. I know that the feelings I have for you now are so much more intense than they were back then, if that makes any sense."

I nod. "It does, I feel it too. I can't explain it, though."

He kisses me again. "Me neither. So I am going to show you, Princess. I have a feeling this is going to be amazing. Are you ready?" I squeak out a, "Yes." He slowly takes off my boots, one at a time, and gently massages each foot. He then stands and holds out his hand, helping me stand in front of him. He lifts my t-shirt over my head. Slowly, he kisses and licks along my neck. He reaches around and unhooks my bra, pulling the straps off my arms one at a time and following each one with light kisses. I feel like I am on fire. I reach down to undo the button on my skirt, but he grabs my wrists and looks up at me.

"I have waited a very long time for this, Princess, we are going to take our time. I am going to touch and kiss every beautiful inch of your body, and you, my dear, are going to sit back and enjoy every pleasurable second."

Holy hell, who could argue with that? I don't think I have ever been more turned on by someone's words in my whole life. I couldn't do anything but whimper. He unbuttons my skirt and lets it fall to the floor. Then, he hooks his fingers in the thin straps of my lace panties and slowly pulls them down to my feet. I lift my feet, one at a time, out of them. He picks me up, carries me to the bed, and gently lays me in the center.

"Do not move your arms, leave them up here," he whispers as he raises my arms above my head.

He sits back on his heels and runs his eyes up and down my body. I should feel self-conscious, lying there naked in front of him staring at me, but the look in his eyes makes me feel beautiful, like I'm the only woman he could ever want.

"You have no idea how fucking beautiful you are, do you? Since you have been back, I don't think there has been a second I am with you that I am not hard and wanting you. Just thinking about you turns me on." He starts to kiss me softly and it grows into something demanding and hungry. He kisses down to my breasts, licking and sucking on one nipple while he teases the other between his fingers.

"Kyle. Please." I am not sure what I am asking for, but he didn't leave time for me to think about it. He kisses down my stomach to each hip, running his hand from my feet up my legs. When he gets to my thighs, he slowly pushes my legs apart and lowers his head between them until I can feel his breath on my clit. He looks me in the eyes, smiles, and then brings his mouth down on me, simultaneously thrusting two fingers inside.

"Oh my God." He licks and sucks my clit while sliding his fingers in and out. I can feel myself getting closer to the edge. I grip the pillow under my head, trying to keep my arms where he wants them. He moves his fingers faster and harder and before I know it, I am screaming his name.

Kyle slowly gets up to remove his jeans and boxers, and oh my, what a sight. He is perfect. Perfect and huge … I had forgotten just how big. He is smiling as he lowers himself over me on the bed. Yeah … I got busted checking him out. Oh well, it's not like he didn't already know how impressive it is. He takes my face in his hands and kisses me passionately. I can feel him rubbing against my entrance. And then slowly, oh so deliciously slowly, he pushes himself all the way inside me, inch by beautiful inch. I close my eyes, inebriated by the amazing feeling of him filling me.

"Keep your eyes open, Amber. Watch me love you." I open my eyes and when I look into his, I see so much love and passion. He starts to move slowly at first then faster, harder. "You feel so good, Amber. See how perfect we fit together?" I can't speak. I am overwhelmed with emotion and a physical pleasure I have never experienced before. I could feel my orgasm building.

"Let go with me, Princess," he groans in my ear and my whole body explodes.

"Kyle … I love you." He thrusts in and out three more times, and I can feel him pulsating through his release.

"Oh, fuck … I love you, too, Princess."

We lie there, tangled in each other, until we catch our breath.

"That was amazing," he says, giving me a quick kiss. Then, up gets up, blows out the candles, and lays back down, wrapping me in his arms, my head resting against his chest. I never want this moment to end. Everything with him feels natural and more intense than anything I have ever experienced. He is it for me. There will never be anyone else.

"What are you thinking about?" he asks as he kisses my forehead

"How happy I am in your arms."

"That's good to hear because I like you in my arms."

"I have been thinking... we spend so much time together anyway, maybe you might want to move in here?" He doesn't answer right away and I start to get nervous. It's too soon to ask. I'm pushing. I should have known better. I risk looking up at him, but his eyes are closed. "I understand if it's—"

He cut me off with a kiss before I could finish. "Of course I want to move in here with you. I've wanted to suggest it since the first night I stayed here, but I was afraid to push you." We both laugh.

"So, should we borrow Paul's truck tomorrow and get you moved in?"

"Abso-fucking-lutely," Kyle growls as he rolls me over and we make love again.

CHAPTER
Eight

Kyle

I AM ON top of the world. Last night, making love to Amber again for the first time, was worth the wait. I was actually more nervous last night than I was the first time we were together. But, it was better than I could imagine. I don't think I will ever get enough of that woman. I can't believe that she wants me to move in. I have been wanting to bring that up since the first night I stayed here with her, but I was afraid I would scare her away. After all, she is the one who wanted to take things slow.

Once we finally made it out of bed this morning, I texted Paul to see if he could help move a few of my things. Luckily, I don't have much. Amber also mentions that Paul and Holly have been looking for a different place. It works out perfectly.

I pull up to the bar and Paul is waiting, leaning on his truck.

"Hey, man, how's it going?" he asks with a sly grin. He knows I've been wanting to bring up moving in with Amber. He kept telling me to relax and slow down.

"Couldn't be better. And, before you give me shit, she asked me. I never mentioned it." I smile and head up the back stairs.

It doesn't take long to pack my clothes in a couple suitcases. The furniture can stay. Everything else fits into about four boxes. After we put everything in the back of the truck, we go inside the bar for a quick beer.

"I was thinking, if you and Holly want the apartment upstairs, it's yours, rent free." I hand him his beer.

"Really, man? That would be great. We've been trying to save up to buy a house in the next year or so. Thanks! Holly is going to be thrilled."

"No problem."

"So, when are you proposing?" he teases. I flip him off. Of course I won't tell him that it's all I can think about. I don't want to be accused of growing a vagina. But, I'm pretty sure a proposal would definitely be pushing Amber too quickly. I throw our empties away and we head out.

We got back to the house and Paul and I unload the truck and bring everything upstairs. We went out back to fire up the grill and see what the girls were up to. Earlier, we had decided to have a cook out, so Amber and Holly have been having 'girl time' while we were away. By the looks of the almost empty pitcher of Appletini's and the giggling girls lounged out on the chairs, I think it's safe to say they haven't been up to much.

Laying there, in a tight tank top and short jean shorts, she looks amazing. All I can think about is hauling her ass upstairs and burying myself inside her. Just the thought has me straining against my zipper. I lean down and kiss her forehead. She grabs my head and brings my ear to her lips and whispers in the most seductive voice I have ever heard, "Last night and this morning when you made love to me was amazing, but I want to know what it's like when you fuck me."

I look in her eyes to see if she was just playing around. She isn't. The want in her eyes is clear. Then, she mouths, "Now." That's all I need. I throw her over my shoulder cave man style, tell Paul and Holly we will be back in a few minutes, and run upstairs to our bedroom.

I close the door, set her on her feet, and back her up against the wall. "Do you have any idea what you do to me, Princess?" She nods, unbuttons her shorts, and pulls them and her panties off in one move. Holy shit, I love this woman. She grabs my hand and brings it between her legs.

"If it's anything like what you do to me, then yes, I have an idea." I plunge two fingers into her wet, tight heat. She gasps and drops her head back against the wall. She unbuttons my jeans and pushes my pants and boxers off my hips. I reach around and cup her ass in my hands, lifting her off the floor. Her legs immediately wrap tightly around my waist and I slam myself into her.

"Is this what you had in mind?" She was right, making love to her slowly and sweetly is amazing, but this... this is mind blowing.

"Yes ... yes!" I can feel her tighten around me as she screams my name. I explode inside of her, harder than I ever have before. I turn us around and slide us down the wall before my legs give out. She looks up and smiles at me

"I liked the slow and sweet, but I think the fast and rough is my favorite."

I laugh. "Woman, you are going to be the death of me. We better get cleaned up, we have guests."

I look down at Amber's face as we walk outside and notice how badly she is blushing. It is so cute and sexy at the same time. Knowing Paul and Holly as I do, though, it is about to get worse.

"Hope you don't mind me throwing on the steaks. You guys sounded a little busy," Paul says to us, trying not to laugh as Holly slaps him on the back of the head. I look over at Amber. Even though she is as red as a beet, she's smiling and laughing right along with them.

We all have a great night just hanging out, eating, drinking and laughing. A lot. It feels so good to sit here with the love of my life and two of my best friends. Life doesn't get much better than this. A few years ago, I never would have imagined this would be my life. As much as I enjoy performing with the band, it did not take me long to realize the life of a rock star was not for me. I enjoy my privacy way too much. I enjoy being in a small town. And, I probably wouldn't have Amber back if I had stayed in L.A.

I look over at Paul. He smiles at me and lifts his beer, as if he knows what I'm thinking. He was lost like I was when we met. He found Holly after he moved back here with me and I can tell he is much happier now. Just like I was glad that he found his happiness, I know he feels the same.

Amber

OF COURSE tonight, of all nights, the bar is packed. Holly and Kyle hounded me all day about singing and I finally gave in. Now, I'm regretting that decision. I make my way to the bar. "Two shots of tequila please, Paul," I ask with a nervous smile. I don't think I can do this. Paul puts the shots in front of me with a wink and goes to help the other customers. I take the first one and quickly tip it back. As I go to grab the second, I see Darcie heading my way. This should be good. Before she gets to me, I quickly down the second shot. I am going to need it, for two reasons now.

"Hi, Amber, how are you?" she asks, a fake smile plastered to her face

"Just fine, thanks."

"I saw you standing here and thought I would come give you a little friendly advice."

"And what would that be Darcie?" I ask as I roll my eyes. This should be good.

"You might as well just give up now. You just don't have what it takes to keep a man like Kyle. You're just, too ... plain." This girl is really pissing me off. Normally, I am not the kind of girl who is outspoken and starts shit. But, the tequila is starting to work its way through my system and I really hate this girl. Like, really.

"And what would you know about keeping a man like Kyle? If memory serves me right, you only had him once. I, on the other hand, have had the privilege of having him multiple times and he keeps coming back for more."

"He wants me. You are just in our way."

"You are just as delusional as your husband. You do know you make yourself look desperate and pathetic, right?" She tries to speak, but I put my hand up and cut her off. "Let me give you some advice, Darcie. It might be better for you to choose a man that doesn't take you as a consolation prize after they can't have me ... maybe then it will work out for you."

"What are you talking about?"

"Oh, sweetie, you didn't know that your ex-husband was in love with me in high school? Only, I didn't want him. And, Kyle, well, he only slept around because I left and he was hurting." She can't hide the anger in her face … or the embarrassment. I can see Paul and Holly staring at us from behind the bar with their mouths wide open. They know I am not one for confrontations, especially in public, but this bitch has pushed my last button. She pulls her phone out and puts it in my face.

"You think Kyle loves you so much? He sure didn't seem to love you a whole lot during this interview. Go ahead, watch it." I take the phone from her hand and look at the screen. It's a YouTube video dated about a year after I left. I'm not sure what this could have to do with me, but I don't think I am going to like it. Here goes nothing. I take a deep breath and press play. There is a lady interviewing Kyle and the guys. Kyle looks wasted. Nothing out of the ordinary has been said so far. I give Darcie a look, and she just points to the screen, so I keep watching.

Interviewer: *Kyle, is there anyone special you attribute your success to?*

Kyle: (Laughs bitterly) *There is actually. The cold, heartless bitch, Amber, who ripped my heart out. I came up with the band name Bleeding Hearts because of her.*

Okay, I have to admit that stings a little. But, really, what is Darcie trying to accomplish with this? There is nothing here that he hasn't already explained and apologized for a million times. I know he was hurting and pissed at me then. She isn't going to accomplish what she hopes by showing me this. I hand her phone back to her with a shrug of my shoulders.

"Your point is? Did you really think by showing me this I was going to dump him and he would come running to you? Even if I wasn't in the picture, he would not give you the time of day."

"You ... you ... you're a bitch!" she spits out, frustrated, and storms off. I just laugh … what else can I do? She really thought that was some smoking gun. I'm thinking the bleach in her hair has gotten into her head. I look over at Paul and Holly who have smiles from ear to ear and are giving me a thumbs-up.

Kyle walks up to tell me it is my turn to sing. I don't bother to tell him about seeing the interview. We both agreed that the past is the past and we are going to focus on our present and future. Whether it's the tequila or the run-in with Darcie, I was no longer nervous about getting up there.

The first couple lines I sing are shaky. I look down and see Kyle. He's looking at me like he wants to eat me alive. My confidence flourishes and I relax. Focusing on him, I belt out the song, no holds barred. And, I have a blast doing it. Next, Kyle and I sing a duet. We end up having a great night. I don't remember the last time I had this much fun.

CHAPTER
Nine

Amber

KYLE WENT into the bar a little early today for deliveries, so I decide to go for a little drive before I head in. There was this old back road I remember that I loved driving along when I was younger. I would drive out there when I needed to think or just be alone, windows rolled down and the radio cranked up as loud as it would go. As I was driving, I started thinking about the youth center back in Atlanta. That is the only thing I regret leaving. I really enjoyed working with the kids and doing something that felt meaningful. It was a great place for kids to come to after school when their parents were still at work so they didn't have to go home alone. We would help them with homework or just give them a place to hang out that was safe and fun. The more I thought about it, the more I realized this town could use a place like that. It would be a great way to do something in honor of my grandparents and to feel like I am doing something fulfilling with my life.

As I was heading back into town, a few miles from KC's, I noticed the old furniture warehouse was for sale. That would be the perfect building for the youth center. I pull into the parking lot to look around.

I walk around the building. There seemed to be quite a bit of land behind it. I could picture a playground area for smaller children, a basketball court, and there even looked like enough space for a field where sports like baseball, football, soccer, and kickball could be played. I looked back to the front of the building and found a window that looked low enough for me to peek through. I could see that, for the most part, the inside was open space. There was a loft area with an office and what looked to be restrooms. Over all, the place was huge and perfect. A plus, there wouldn't need to be many renovations made. I turned as I heard a car pull in the lot behind me. An older man got out of the car and approached me with a smile. He was tall and lanky with short salt and pepper hair. His navy blue suit didn't quite fit in around this town. It looked too expensive, like something Daniel would wear.

"Hi, I'm Mike Weathers of Weather's Realty. Can I help you with something?" He held out his hand and I shook it as I introduced myself.

"Yes actually, I am interested in buying this place."

"Would you like to take a look inside?" He held up a set of keys. I nodded and followed him in.

The place was as perfect as I thought it would be. There was an upstairs loft area that had two large offices, a conference room, and restrooms. There was even a full kitchen and dining area already in place. It would not need much at all to turn this into what I started to envision. It was amazing. Before I knew it, I was signing a contract and writing a check for the deposit. I thanked Mr. Weathers and set a time to meet him next week to close the deal and headed to KC's. I couldn't wait to tell Kyle.

The bar isn't open yet and the only vehicle in the lot is Kyle's truck. I walk around back and use my key to unlock the door. As I walk through the back hall, I see Kyle in his office working at his desk. I lean against the door and just watch him for a few minutes. He is so cute when he is concentrating on something. His face scrunches up and he works his lips back and forth. If it were anybody else, it would probably look silly. But, I swear, this man could make anything look sexy. As if on cue, he looks up and notices me watching him. A slow, sexy smile spreads across his face and my knees go weak.

"How long have you been standing there?" he asks as he puts his hand out for me to walk over to him.

"Long enough," I say as I reach him. He pulls me to sit across his lap. His lips gently brush against mine before he deepens the kiss, sucking at my lips, teasing them apart, and exploring my mouth with his tongue. I can feel him harden beneath me the instant he kisses me. "Excited to see me?" I ask as I wiggle my ass in his lap

"Always, Princess. But, if you keep doing that, I am going to bend you over this desk," he growls in my ear, and it makes me shiver.

"What are you waiting for?" I ask as I wiggle again. He groans and stands up, placing me on my feet as he closes and locks the door to his office. I am leaning back against the desk watching him. He looks at me like a lion stalking his prey; I can't wait for him to catch me.

"Turn around," he says as he stalks closer. I comply. He put his hands on my shoulders and slowly runs them down my arms until he is holding my wrists. He places my hands, palms down, on the desktop. "Don't move them." He grabs the bottom of my jean skirt and pushes it up to my waist. Hooking his fingers into my panties, he slides them down my legs. I hear him unzipping his jeans and pulling them down. He wastes no time. Thank God. One arm snakes around under my shirt and caresses my breasts as the other hand slips between my legs.

"Always so wet for me, Princess," he whispers, then slams his cock into to me. I scream out as he pumps his hips in a furious rhythm.

I love the gentle and sweet Kyle, but I also love this one. The Kyle that seems to want me so much he loses all control. He reaches around and circles my clit with his thumb. I immediately tighten around him, calling his name over and over. He thrusts a couple more times before I feel him swell inside of me, spilling into me as he wraps his arms tightly around me. "I love you so much, Amber. You are everything to me," he says as he kisses my neck.

"I love you, too."

Kyle

I AM sitting at the bar watching Amber. God, I love that woman. All of my friends absolutely love her, and she loves them. Plus, we seemed to pick up like six years wasn't lost between us, and it feels better, like we are stronger together for it. Earlier today, in my office, holy shit! I was just playing around, I wasn't planning on taking her on my desk like that, but she was all for it. It's nice to know that she wants me as badly and as often as I do her.

She told me about her plans to open the youth center, which I think is fantastic. It's nice to see her excited about something she enjoys. She has always been such a loving, caring, and giving person, so it does not surprise me at all that this is something she wants to do. Of course I told her I will be here to help with anything she may need.

She looks over her shoulder, notices I am watching her, and gives me that sexy ass smile of hers. My dick twitches. I must be grinning like an idiot because Holly is smirking at me. "What are you looking at me like that for?"

"No reason, you just look really happy for the first time since I met you. It's nice to see."

"I am very happy, actually." I smile at her as Amber saunters over. I pull her to my lap and kiss her forehead.

"You two are so sugary sweet, you are going to give me a fucking cavity," Holly joked and went to the other side of the bar.

"How's your night going, Princess?"

"Pretty good. I texted a friend I worked with at the youth center in Atlanta to see if they were interested in coming to work for me." She looked a little nervous. I wonder if it's just bringing up Atlanta, or if there is something about this friend I need to worry about.

"What did she say?"

"Well, first, it's not a she. His name is Jackson Cobb and he will be here in a month. We went to school together in Atlanta, he was in charge of the youth center I volunteered at. He is very good at what he does and would be an asset to my center. He has also been a very good friend." She turns to look me in the eye. "And, before you ask, no, we never dated. He asked when we were in college, but I turned him down and told him I would rather be friends. That's what we've been for six years." I trust Amber completely, but I know how beautiful she is in and out. While she may have looked at him as just a friend, he was probably waiting for his chance for it to be something more. I could be wrong, but Jackson Cobb is on my radar. I smile at her and kiss her forehead.

"I'm glad you were able to get him to take the job. I look forward to meeting him. If you like him, I'm sure I will, too."

"Kyle Connor, don't you think you are fooling me with that bullshit for one second. I know what is going through that macho, male brain of yours." My girl knows me all too well.

"And what would that be?" I ask with a chuckle.

"You think that just because he is a man and I am a woman there is no way he is only interested in me as just a friend. And, since he asked me out once six years ago, that he is only hanging around as my friend waiting for his chance to get in my pants." She looks at me and cocks her eyebrow. Well, hell what can I say? She had me.

"Yeah, that pretty much sums it up." I give her an apologetic smile even though I know I'm probably right about this guy.

"You do know that I love you, right? More than I have ever or could ever love any man?" She places a soft kiss on my lips, her voice soft. "You are the man that makes my heart beat faster when you walk in the room. That makes my stomach fill with a thousand butterflies with just a look." Another soft kiss. "So, no matter what Jackson may or may not feel for me, it doesn't matter. You own my heart, my body, and my soul. When I look at him, I see a friend. Anything more than that, on my part, is absolutely impossible." She crashes her lips against mine and kisses me so intensely, I forget we are in the middle of a crowded bar.

"Princess, I never doubted your feelings about me. I trust you. I am just not sure I trust any man who has feelings for you. If I didn't have you, I would do anything and everything I could to make you mine. There is not another woman on this earth like you. I can't blame a man for falling for you. But, the minute he steps out of line, I will put him back over it."

"Promise you will be nice to him unless he gives you a legitimate reason, and I promise to let you throw his ass back over the line if he crosses it. Deal?"

"Deal." God I love this woman. Though, I still have a feeling I am going to be kicking this guy's ass.

CHAPTER
Ten

Amber

THIS LAST month has been so busy. I finalized the purchase of the warehouse for the youth center, which I am really excited about. I really want this to be a place where the kids love to come to and parents feel safe sending their children. I was putting up some of the money myself, but also received quite a few donations from people and businesses throughout our community. I set up a program with the high school and the community college for internships. A few trainers from the hospital volunteered time to teach a couple CPR classes a month to the kids. We are set to accept children from infants to seventeen. Even though there will be fees for daycare or after school care services, they will be a lot cheaper than traditional places. We also have a fund in place for families who cannot afford to pay for the services but need them.

Kyle has a few friends in construction, so he was able to get a lot of the improvements and changes we need either donated or extremely discounted. We had the entire back of the property fenced in, a playground area with swings, a jungle gym, a couple slides, and the section for toddlers with smaller equipment. Which is one of my favorite parts. A grill and picnic tables are arranged around the grassy area, as well. On the other side, we built a basketball court. There is a volleyball court complete with beach sand and enough field area set up to play soccer, football, or kickball.

Since the inside was completely open aside from the kitchen and dining areas, we had to create different rooms. A nursery room, a toddler room, and a pre-school room were designed so that the smaller children could have everything they needed all in one room away from older kids. There are also several rooms for different activities such as music, art, and classroom-type rooms for tutoring. We also added a common room with a pool table, ping pong table, chess, checkers, and other board games.

Currently, I'm in the art room putting away stacks of paper. I bend over, loading reams of paper in the bottom of the cabinet when I feel a pair of strong arms wrap around my waist. I slowly stand up.

"That is one sexy ass you have there, Princess." He ground himself against my ass. "Can you feel what it did to me?" he growled in my ear. I was seriously thinking about taking him up to my office and having my way with him. He was kissing and licking down my neck.

"Mmmm ... how about you take that hard co—" All of a sudden we hear someone clear their voice. We both spin around and there stands Jackson Cobb. Now, I may not have romantic feelings for him, but I'm still a woman and can appreciate a good looking man. Jax is the opposite of Kyle when it comes to looks. He's a little over six-foot with a broad, lean body. You can tell he works out, but he doesn't have the definition like Kyle does. He has short, honey-blond hair, pine green eyes, and a smile that would make any woman swoon.

"I'm sorry ... I didn't mean to interrupt anything. I yelled for ya, but you must not have heard me." He walks over and holds his hand out to Kyle first. "You must be Kyle. I'm Jax. It's nice to finally meet you." Kyle smiles and shakes his hand.

"Jax, good to meet you." Okay ... so far, so good. For a month, I've been wondering how this meeting was going to go. Kyle's never really been the jealous type. But, for some reason, the idea of Jax being here brings out his jealousy. Jax comes over to me and pulls me into a hug. I swear, I can hear Kyle growling.

"It is so good to see you, Amber. Atlanta wasn't the same after you left." He still had that dazzling smile on his face.

"I'm glad you were willing to take this job. I am so relieved to have someone as good as you here to help me run this place."

"Anything for you. How about showing me where my office is?" We all walk out of the art room toward the stairs just as Paul comes in the front doors. After I introduce him and Jax to each other, he says he needs me outside to show him where to put the new sign. Kyle says he would show Jax to his office for me. I gave him a look, begging him to be nice, but I have a feeling he is going to make sure Jax knows exactly who I belong to. And, by the looks that were exchanged between Paul and Kyle, I think Paul knows it, too. Normally, that behavior would piss me off. Coming from Kyle, though, it tends to turn me on. I watch Kyle lead Jax up the stairs and pray everyone will act like the adults they are and behave.

Kyle

I AM not really a jealous guy, usually, but there is something about the way Jax looks at Amber that makes me feel the need to mark my territory. Yes, I know I sound like a douche, but I have no control over these feelings. He just has this look to him. You know the type, the pretty boy who is used to getting what he wants. He may fool Amber, but he is not fooling me. At all. I know he wants my girl, but he is sadly mistaken if he thinks he can have her.

"Here ya go, this is yours." I open the door for him and wave him inside. He looks around and puts his bag down. He looks like he wants to say something but isn't sure how or what to say. I figure I would start. "Amber is really glad you took this job, she said you did a great job back in Atlanta."

"I am happy to come out here to help, I've missed having her around. She is a great woman, and one of my best friends until she left." Okay … he brought up the friend word, so I am just going to ask what I need to ask and get it all out there. The sooner I know where he stands, the better.

"I keep getting the feeling that you want a little more than friendship from Amber." At least he looked a little embarrassed

"I'm not going to lie to you. I have been in love with her for a long time, but she made it clear that she only wants to be friends. That's what I've been." I can't blame the guy. Who wouldn't fall for her?

"I appreciate the honesty. I can understand falling for her. She is a total package. Just so we are on the same page, you are not going after her in anyway, correct?" He smiles, but it doesn't quite reach his eyes.

"I respect her too much to try to go after her. She already told me no. Plus, I am not the kind of guy that tries to split people up." I give him a smile and a nod. I feel better. He seems like an okay guy, but only time will tell. I head for his door and before I can get all the way out, he starts to speak again.

"Make no mistake, though, Kyle. When you fuck things up with her and she gives me any indication that she has changed her mind about me, I will take my chance."

"I know how lucky I am to have her. I will not fuck it up. She's it for me. There is no one else. Save yourself a lot of lonely nights and calloused hands. Find your own girl." It took all of my self-control to walk out without kicking the living shit out of this mother fucker. I don't care what he says, he is going to do everything he can to wedge in between us. Unless I want to help him along and come out of this looking like a crazy possessive asshole, I am going to have to keep my cool. I head outside to check on Amber and Paul.

Looks like they are just finishing up with the sign. It looks great in big, bold, black letters that read *Oakville Community Youth Center*. At the bottom, in beautiful script, it says, "In Memory of Gene and Ima Lewis." Gene and Ima were two of the greatest people. Amber loved them more than anything and so did I. I never knew any of my grandparents and since Amber and I were attached at the hip since we were toddlers, they treated me like a grandson. Mrs. Lewis always said Amber and I were meant for each other. She was so disappointed when I came back from Atlanta and told her Amber was engaged. She said to be patient, that she would come back to me someday. I didn't believe her at the time, but, as always, she was right. I smiled and said a silent, "Thank you," to them both. They never interfered in anyone's business, but I have a feeling that somehow from heaven they played a huge role in bringing Amber back to me. They would be so proud of what she is doing with this youth center.

She looks so beautiful in the sunshine, laughing with Paul. She has been working so hard lately on the center, I think she is due for a little break and a walk down memory lane. Plus, I have something very important to discuss with her and now is as good a time as any.

I thought about waiting a while longer, but I have loved this girl my whole life. If it's at all possible I love her more after our separation. I know how dark, lonely, and painful my life is without her in it. And, because of that, I am not wasting any more time.

As soon as I get close enough, I pull her into my arms and kiss her gently. I just can't get enough of her. I hope this feeling never goes away. "That sign is amazing, babe. I love the dedication at the bottom," I say as I kiss her on the forehead. She gives me a sad smile.

"I wish they could be here to see this place. I miss them both so much." I hate seeing her sad, especially when this is something I can't fix.

"I know you do, so do I. They may not be here, but they see what you are doing and they are very proud of you." She smiles a little brighter at those words and it warms my heart.

"Thank you. I am going to go check on Jax." She kisses my cheek and heads toward the door.

When Amber goes inside to check on Jax, I fill Paul in on what I want to do and ask him to help me out. Once he has his instructions and is on his way, I go up to get my girl.

I'm walking up the stairs to Amber's office when I hear the two of them talking. I really try not to eavesdrop, but I hear my name, and well, I just can't help it. Yeah, I know it was a shitty thing to do, but I never said I was perfect. I lean up against the wall outside her door.

"I remember the way you were in Atlanta ... how can you take him back after he did that to you?"

"Jax ... it was all a misunderstanding. I told you he didn't do anything. I was the one who overreacted and left town without a word. I did that to myself."

"I'm sure you are going to blame yourself for all the booze, drugs, and women he's had over the last six years too, huh?" I really am starting to hate this guy with every fiber of my being.

"Jax, I told you those things because you are my friend and I needed a shoulder. Not so you could throw it in Kyle's face. In a roundabout way, yes I do, and before you say another word, this conversation is done, Jax. I love Kyle; he is not going anywhere. So, back to your cousin coming to town. I'm sure we can find a spot for her when she gets here." That's my girl. I walk in with a huge smile on my face and place a chaste kiss on her lips.

"I think Jax can finish up on his own. Right, man?" I look at Jax, give him a sly grin, and turn back to Amber before she can protest. "You've been working very hard lately and I have a surprise planned for you." She smiles and starts grabbing her things.

"Okay, you should have everything you need to lock up, Jax. I will see you tomorrow," she says over her shoulder

"I'll be fine, have a good time." Amber can't see that the look on his face doesn't match the tone in his voice. He isn't happy about her leaving with me. I can't resist. I give him my best fuck you smile and pull Amber closer.

CHAPTER
Eleven

Amber

KYLE HELPS me in his truck, but before he closes the door he gives me a kiss that has me wanting to straddle him in his truck. Of course, he knows what he is doing. He laughs as he breaks the kiss and shuts my door. I hope bringing Jax here wasn't a mistake. I can feel the tension between the two of them from a mile away. I'm proud of Kyle though, he is handling it very well. So far. I'll just have to make sure Jax knows there is nothing more than a friendship between us. I asked him here because he was very good at running the center in Atlanta and I know he will be a huge asset here. I just need to make sure that nothing will come between Kyle and me again. "Are you going to tell me where we are going?"

"No, that would ruin the whole part about it being a surprise." He gave me his sexy smile and a wink. I don't really like surprises, and he knows it. So, maybe, I can get it out of him. I unhook my seatbelt, lift the console, and slide into the middle seat next to him. I find the other seat belt, click it in place, and rest my hand on his thigh and my head on his shoulder. I start running my hand up his thigh over his rock hard abs and along his chest.

"Could I persuade you to give me a hint?" I whisper in his ear. I feel him suck in a breath.

"You are an evil woman ... you know that, right?" He looks over quickly before turning his attention back to the road.

"Trust me, there is nothing evil about what I am planning on doing to you. In fact, I think you will find it very pleasurable ... mind blowing, even," I whisper in the most seductive voice I can. I must be doing something right because his chest is rising and falling, rapidly. If that isn't enough, the obvious growing bulge between his legs is a dead giveaway. I love that I can affect this man with only a few words and simple touches. It makes me feel desirable and sexy. He is trying to play it as cool as possible, but he isn't doing a very good job.

"Wh ... what was it you had in mind?" Oh yeah, he knows exactly what I have in mind. As turned on as he is by the idea, I bet if he was in charge of guarding the nation's nuclear launch codes, before this was over, they would be in my hands. At this point, I don't care where we are going anymore. He is like a hormonal teenager in a whore house. I reach down and unhook his belt, undo the button, and slowly pull down the zipper of his jeans. I smile up at him. I love it when he doesn't wear boxers.

"Did you forget something when you got dressed this morning?" I tease. He quickly looks down at me and smiles.

"No, I didn't forget anything. Fucking you whenever I want is much easier with less clothing in the way." If I could keep him naked twenty-four hours a day, I would. I slide my hand into his jeans and wrap my hand around his hard cock, ease it out of its confines, and begin to leisurely stroke it. I look up at him again and slowly lick my lips. He takes a ragged breath. I lower my head and take him into my mouth.

"Fuck!" Kyle growls the minute I run my tongue along his length then back up. I tease his head a little before taking him in again, sucking as hard as I can. "Oh, Amber, that it so good," he moans. I feel the truck come to a stop and Kyle puts it into park. We are either pulled over or at our destination. I really don't care. I am enjoying the look of pleasure on Kyle's face too much. He keeps one hand gripped on the steering wheel so tightly that I can see his knuckles turning white. The other hand is wrapped around my hair just enough to control the depth and speed of my mouth on his cock. "Amber! I'm going to come, baby," he growls. I feel his whole body tighten before he starts spilling down my throat. I kiss and lick him a little bit more, then put him back in his

71

jeans. When I look up at him, he has his head back, his eyes closed, and one hell of a smile on his face. God, I love to see him smile, especially when I know I put it there. I just lay there with my head in his lap looking up at him while he runs his hands through my hair.

Being with only him and Daniel, I don't have a lot of experience with sex. Daniel was very vanilla, always missionary, nothing changed. EVER. He was so plain, it was almost impossible to get him to kiss my neck. Like he was programmed, lips touch lips and that's it. The only thing he ever seemed to pay a lot of attention to was my breasts. Normally, that's not a bad thing. But, I hated it. Everything else was so neglected that I cringed every time he tried to touch my boobs. From start to finish, sex was over in like thirty minutes, including his sad idea of foreplay. He never said anything during, no noises, nothing. I swear, he didn't even breathe heavy. When he was done, he would get right up, get dressed, and get back to what he was doing before. God, thinking about it now ... why in the hell did I stay with him? But again, where sex was concerned, I didn't know it could be different. Kyle was my first, I was his, and he was nowhere near as skilled back then as he is now. Even at eighteen and inexperienced, it was better than with Daniel. I always chalked that up to the feelings. I knew I didn't love Daniel like I did Kyle.

"That was amazing, Princess. But, I'm afraid it was all for nothing. This is where we're going." He smiles and kisses my forehead. Before I look to see where we are, I look in his eyes.

"Well, since I didn't get my hints from you, I guess you are just going to have to show me what your mouth can do when it's between my legs later." He chuckles. I can see by the look on his face that he likes when I talk like that to him. For some reason, I'm feeling bold. Maybe it is watching how easily I can make Kyle come apart by taking control.

"That is definitely something I can do. But, first ... your surprise." He caresses my cheek then turns my head to look out the windshield.

We are at Reed Lake. We used to come here all the time when we were teenagers. This is where Kyle first made love to me. The lake itself is fairly small, but it's beautiful. The water is almost clear, there are cattails along the banks, and some of the most beautiful old oak trees hanging over the lake. It is very secluded back here. Of all the times we have been here, I have never seen anyone else. On the other side of the lake in a clearing there was a blanket set up with a cooler and a metal fire pit. I can't believe he did all this. It is so romantic.

"Do you remember this place?" Kyle asks shyly.

"Of course I do, how could I forget it? We have made some amazing memories here together." I kiss him softly on his lips.

"How about we go make some more tonight," he says as he nips my earlobe.

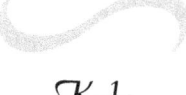

Kyle

I LEAD her to the clearing. As she sits down on the blanket, I pour us both a glass of champagne. I need to remember to take my time and stick to my plan so that this night is perfect for her. After her little performance in the truck, it is going to be very difficult to keep myself under control. She is always surprising me in one way or another. Tonight it's my turn to surprise her. As soon as I get the fire going, I turn around and see that she is watching me with a cute little smirk on her face.

"What are you smiling about?"

"Besides that sexy body of yours? I was thinking of the first time you brought me here for a picnic."

That first picnic was the night we both lost our virginity. Even though it was probably one of the best nights of my life, I didn't know what the hell I was doing. I was nervous as hell. So much so, I threw up twice before I even picked her up. At least this time around I know what I am doing.

"I enjoyed myself that night, but the fact that I didn't know shit about pleasing you must have been very disappointing for you."

"It was perfect. You forget, I didn't know anything either."

I am really going to have to do something nice for Paul. Actually, Holly is probably responsible for all of this. It's perfect. I pull out a couple sandwiches and hand one to Amber. She takes it and smiles. I can see how happy she is. I only hope to keep seeing that happiness on her face for the rest of our lives. We talk while we finish the sandwiches. By the time we finish, the sun is setting, so I grab the acoustic guitar that Paul hid for me on the other side of the tree. As soon as she sees it, she shakes her head. I look up to see she has tears in her eyes. I start to panic. Did I do something wrong? Does she know what I am planning?

I quickly kneel next to her.

"Princess, what's wrong? Why are you crying?"

"Nothing is wrong. I am not upset. This is all just so romantic and perfect. These are happy tears, I promise." I can't help myself; I kiss her like I have never kissed her before. I try to put everything I feel for her in that kiss. When I pull back, she is breathing heavily and I am so hard, it hurts. But, I'm sticking to my plan.

"I love you, Princess. I wanted to write a song for you, but I just couldn't seem to get the words down on paper. I know this isn't as romantic, but this song always makes me think of you." I sit in front of her, get my guitar situated, and began singing *Tangled Up in You* by Staind.

I finish and set the guitar aside. Tears are rolling down her cheeks and I wipe them away with my fingers.

"I want you to know how much you mean to me. You coming back into my life made me the happiest man in the world. I finally feel like I have just about everything I have ever wanted in my life. I know we haven't been back together very long, but we have known each other our whole lives. Everything with you feels right, perfect; like we are two puzzle pieces that fit together." I reach into my pocket and pull out the little black velvet box and open it in front of her. She gasps. "Amber, I want to love you, make you happy, make you laugh, kiss away your tears, and be the father to your children. I want to hold you every night when we go to sleep, wake up and kiss that beautiful face every morning. Will you marry me?"

CHAPTER
Twelve

Amber

I GASP, COMPLETELY shocked and overwhelmed with emotion from the most beautiful song I've ever heard. He gave that to me, sang it to me. Now, kneeling before me is Kyle holding the most gorgeous ring I have ever seen. It's a two carat, princess cut, solitaire on a gold band. I know what's coming next. I know what I will say. I just can't believe he is doing this so soon.

His proposal, his words, are heartfelt and sincere. I can't feel it, see it when I look in his eyes. He means every word and I'm speechless. I can't get the words out, but I can definitely envision spending the rest of my life with him. There is no doubt in my mind.

"Baby, we don't have to do anything right away. We can wait as long as you want for a wedding. I just want to know that you want all the same things. I'm really not trying to push you."

"Yes," is all I can get out, the tears falling fast and hard.

"Yes what, Princess?"

"Yes, of course I will marry you. I love you so much. You make me so happy, Kyle. I have wanted to marry you since I was five years old."

"You have just made me incredibly happy." He takes my hand in his and places the ring on my finger. It fits perfectly. He brings my hand to his lips and kisses where he just placed the ring. "And, now that you've gotten your surprise, I think it's time I make good on what I owe you." He grabs my other hand and pulls me closer to the fire, telling me to lie down.

He's not even touching me, but the look on his face is full of pleasurable promises. Every nerve ending in my body tingles with excitement. He leisurely begins to unbutton my shirt, causing me to regret my wardrobe choice this morning. He's not veering away from his plans to be romantic and take his time. I'm almost ready to scream for him to rip the damn shirt off. Once the last button is undone, he pushes the shirt open and slides it off my arms. He starts to trail kisses from my forehead, down my cheek, to my ear, along my neck, and when he finally gets to the swell of my breasts, I am ready to explode. He kisses and licks the mound not covered by my satin bra as his hand reaches around to unhook it. I lift my arms and he pulls the bra off, tossing it aside. His hands cup my breasts and trail down to the waistband of my jeans. He opens the button, glides the zipper down, and slips them off, tossing them to join the growing pile of discarded clothes.

I lay there in nothing but a pair of lace panties while he sits back on his heels and lets his eyes wander from my head to my feet and back again very slowly. "Absolutely beautiful," he says in a husky whisper. He lifts his shirt over his head and gives me a sexy grin when he notices me looking at the delicious V shape at his hips.

He slowly pulls my lace panties off as he leans down and brings his lips to mine, hard. So hard, I can feel it in my toes. His lips move from mine, down my neck to my breasts. He licks and sucks each nipple until I'm writhing beneath him. He eases lower, circling my belly button with his tongue while his hands are on my thighs, pushing my legs apart.

When his warm tongue flicks my clit, my whole body feels like it is on fire. He starts teasingly slow at first, licking and sucking, never taking his eyes of mine. When he picks up the pace, he thrusts two of his fingers inside me.

"Oh …" I close my eyes, the intense pleasure that building. His mouth leaves my slick flesh.

"Open your eyes, Princess … I want you to watch me make you come." As soon as I open them, he devours me again and my orgasm hits me like a tidal wave. He slowly moves up my body, placing kisses as he moves, until his cock is rubbing against my entrance. His lips crash down on mine at the same time he slams into me, causing me to cry out. I wrap my legs around his hips, trying to pull him closer.

Kyle slows his pace as he leans down so his lips are against my ear, his warm breath sending shivers down my spine.

"I am never letting you go again." His voice is straining as he tries to get the words out. All the emotions I am feeling are apparent in his voice. "I am going to spend every day for the rest of my life loving you."

Between his words, his deep voice, and his cock sliding in and out of me, I am about to explode, again. He links our fingers together, brings our arms over my head, and begins to thrust his hips harder, faster.

"Oh. God. Kyle!" I can feel myself tighten around him, causing his release.

"Fuck. Baby!" As soon as we catch our breath, Kyle rolls onto his back, pulling me next to him so my head rests on his chest.

"I love you, Kyle," I say as I turn to look up at him. He smiles down at me.

"I love you too, Princess. With everything I am." We lie there wrapped in each other's arms for a long time before getting up to head home. What a perfect night.

Kyle

ON SUNDAY, since the bar is closed, we decide to have a cookout at the house. Holly is calling it an engagement party, and since Amber has been so busy with the opening of the center, Holly was put in charge. I was told to do whatever she needed. I knew right then I was in for it. I love Holly like a sister, she's great and she makes my best friend happy, but there were a few times this week I wanted to lock her in a closet. I had asked her why we needed all the crap she was getting, and after she gave me a look that almost knocked me on my ass, she said, "She is a special person who deserves a special engagement party that she will remember for the rest of her life."

Well shit, I couldn't argue with that. She was right. Amber deserves the best. After that, I didn't complain anymore.

When I woke up this morning, I heard voices downstairs. I realized I must have slept later than usual. The guys and I hung out at the bar for a while after closing last night, so I didn't get home until three-thirty this morning. I rolled out of bed and jumped in the shower. I put on a plain, white, V-neck t-shirt with a pair of jeans and my favorite worn, brown cowboy boots. These boots have definitely seen better days, but I love them.

I followed the voices to the kitchen. There was Amber and Holly, cooking a bunch of food for this afternoon. Every time I see her it's like the first time. My heart starts beating faster and harder, my stomach flip-flops, I get this goofy grin on my face, and my dick becomes instantly hard.

"Good morning, ladies," I say as I kiss Amber on the top of her head and head for the coffee pot.

"Morning!" Holly calls out, her attention fixed on peeling potatoes.

"Good morning, handsome. How'd you sleep?" Amber asks as she stands next to me at the counter.

"Pretty good. Looks like you two have been busy. What do you need me to do?"

"Nothing yet. Paul, Angel, and Marcus will be here in an hour or so with the tables and chairs. You can help them when they get here."

"Sounds good. I think I need a kiss from those sweet lips of yours to start my day off right, though." She smiles at me and moves closer. I lean down and crash my lips to hers. As soon as that little whimper leaves her, I'm ready to pick her up and carry her up stairs.

"Okay, lover boy, you need to knock that shit off right now. We have a lot of work to do and you're a distraction. You could always go and get some more beer if you want to help out," Holly says as she pulls Amber out of my arms.

I head down to the bar to grab some beer and ice. By the time I get back the guys were there and we set up the tables and chairs out in the back yard. Holly really did a great job with this party. She even has a small stage set up in the corner so the band can play a little later. She has an area set up for the kids to help keep them busy. There is so much food. The girls made all kinds of salads, vegetables, and appetizers. There is steak, chicken, ribs, hamburgers, and hotdogs to grill. Clark and Marty volunteered to man the grills. Looks like Holly even got a few extra grills. I am glad we did this. It will be nice to see all of our friends together, relaxing and having fun. Ever since my mom moved back to Texas to be close to her sister, I don't see her much. Amber has no family left anymore, so I consider most of the people coming today our family.

People are starting to arrive, so I begin to make my way around to greet them. First, I go over to see Taryn, Marcus's wife, and their four year old son, Chase. Taryn and Marcus have been together since they were in high school. Chase is a spitting image of his dad, except for Chase's jet-black Mohawk. He gives me a quick high five and is off and running.

I spot Clark and his two boys, Skylar who's six and Mason who's nine. Clark's been raising his boys by himself for the last five and a half years. His girlfriend just up and took off one day. She said she didn't want to be tied down. He is one hell of a dad, though; always doing things with those boys. Clark's mom takes care of the boys when he works. They are very polite and well-behaved. They both say hello and thank me for inviting them before heading off to play. Clark makes his way to start working on the grill.

Marty walks by me and yells a greeting on his way to the grills. I look over to Amber and see her talking to his wife, Anna, and their two kids, sixteen year old Makenna and twenty year old Matthew. I smile and wave. My smile quickly fades when I see Jax and his cousin, Leena, walk in. He leans down and kisses Amber on the cheek. I want to knock his head off his shoulders. He knows what he's doing because he looks in my direction and smirks at me. I really can't stand that guy; he doesn't even try to hide the fact that he is trying to get my girl. And that cousin of his? She is a real piece of work. She moved down here to work at the youth center. Jax said she was so good with kids and loved working with them. After one shift, Amber said it wasn't going to work out. Of course, she felt bad and begged me to hire her at the bar. Of course, I can't say no to her. Leena has only been working two days, but I can already tell she is trouble. The customers love Leena … especially those of the male variety. She looks like a human Barbie doll, complete with long blond hair, blue eyes, and huge fake boobs. She definitely attracts a lot of attention. Problem is … the only attention she seems to want is mine. At first, I brushed the flirting off as innocent. But, the more it happened, the less I could ignore it. I told Amber right away. I did not want any misunderstandings. Then, I sat Leena down to try to explain that it had to stop. Well, that didn't go quite like I thought it would.

I was sitting at my desk when there was a knock on the door. I knew it was Leena, I had asked Holly to send her in. I needed to discuss the fact that her flirting had gotten out of hand and it needed to stop. She sauntered in, putting a little too much sway in her hips. She was an attractive girl. If this would have been happening before Amber came back, things may have been different. With Amber in my life, no other woman gets my attention like that. Sure, I can appreciate a beautiful woman, but that's as far as it goes. I point to the chair on the other side of my desk. She takes a seat.

"I am going to get right to the point, Leena. You know I am engaged to Amber, yet you are continually inappropriate with the way you flirt with me. I need you to stop." I expected to see embarrassment in her expression and was floored when I saw amusement. She actually had a grin on her face.

"I am attracted to you and I know you think I am attractive, so what's the problem?" Did she really just say that? What part of 'I am engaged' does she not get?

"How can there not be a problem? I am engaged to Amber. I love Amber. Yes, you are a pretty girl, but I am not interested in you." She still smiled like I was speaking in opposites.

"What she doesn't know won't hurt her," she said with a giggle. You have got to be fucking kidding me. What is it with me and attracting bunny boiling crazies?

"Yeah, but see ... I would know, and I am not that kind of guy. Plus, I'm your boss."

"You might be engaged now, and you might love her, but does she love you? She spends a lot of time with Jax, and I know for a fact he wants her. So, I will cool it for now. Just know I'm here when you come to your senses." With that, she stood up and walked out of my office.

I think it's time that they both know that Amber and I are together, and that is how it is going to stay.

I walk up to Amber and pull her close to me. "Hey there, beautiful. How is my wife-to-be doing?"

"I am doing great husband-to-be, how about you?" she asks, smiling up at me.

"There is something I need to show you, Princess," I say to her with a smile. I look at Jax and Leena. "Would you two excuse us for a bit?" I grab Amber's hand and lead her into the house. On the way through the kitchen, Holly tries to stop us. "I promise I will have her back down in twenty minutes!" I yell as I continue up the stairs.

As soon as we get into the bedroom, I shut the door and lock it. I back her against the wall. I've been wanting her all day and seeing that asshole kiss her cheek makes the need for me to be inside her that much greater. By the look of desire in her beautiful brown eyes, I would say she wants this just as bad.

"Princess, I have wanted to be inside you all day. I can't wait any longer." That must be all she needs to hear. She kicks off her sandals and undresses.

"You better get those jeans off, we have a yard full of guests." God, I love this about her. She always wants me as badly as I want her. Anytime, anywhere, any way. It makes her so much hotter. I quickly drop my jeans as she reaches her arms around my neck and crashes her lips to mine. I bend down and grab her ass as she wraps her legs around me and I lift her up. She reaches down between us, grabs my cock in her hand, and lines it up with her slick entrance.

"Sorry, baby, this isn't going to be slow and sweet," I tell her before slamming her down on me. Her sexy moans add fuel to the fire. She digs her nails into my shoulders.

"Kyle!" Her body clamps around me so hard it makes me explode inside her.

"Fuuuck, Princess." I groan. I turn around so my back is to the wall and slide us down to the floor. "I love you," I whisper in her ear.

"I love you, too," she says back.

How did I get so lucky to have this amazing woman for the rest of my life?

CHAPTER
Thirteen

Amber

I CLEAN UP in the bathroom and head back down to the kitchen to see what Holly needed earlier. When I walk into the kitchen, Holly and Taryn look at me and start laughing.

"What's so funny?" I ask, not able to keep the smile off my face.

"The fact that Kyle just walked through here with the same just-fucked smile," Holly says through her laughter.

"Yes, you both look quite happy," Taryn giggles.

"You're just jealous," I say with a wink. I grab a bowl of potato salad and make my way outside.

Everyone looks like they are having a great time. Mr. and Mrs. Thompson are over at a table eating and chatting with Marty's wife, Anna. Both of their kids are working at the youth center and doing a great job. Their daughter, Makenna, volunteers during the week through one of her school programs. She also works on the weekend doing whatever is needed of her. She plans on becoming an elementary school teacher. Her brother, Matthew, plans to be a high school P.E. teacher and coach. It works out great for both of us. Not only does he get credits for school by working here, but he runs all of our sport activities. Even today when they should be relaxing, I find them in the middle of all the kids playing and keeping them busy. Anna and Marty even come in a couple days a week to volunteer. Anna usually helps out in the nursery. She says it has been so long since she held babies, and she misses it. Marty usually has a fun cooking project. The other day he had the kids make their own mini pizzas. They thought it was the coolest thing ever.

This center has become more than I imagined. So many people are truly happy to help make it a great place for this community. Even the guys in Bleeding Hearts come over and help out with music classes. So far, everyone I have hired is working out well, with the exception to Leena. Jax said she worked with him before and was great with kids. She didn't last a day with me. First, she came in so inappropriately dressed, I almost asked her to go home and change. She wore a top so low-cut I was afraid if she bent over her girls would just flop right out to say hi. And the shorts, my God, her ass cheeks were peeking out just a tad even without bending over. She looks like she should be working at a Hooters, not at a youth center. But, Jax said she is great with kids, so I gave her a chance. She acted like the kids were diseased and she didn't want to get too close. The only productive thing she did was flirt. None of the men were comfortable with her and all of the women hated her. I had no choice but to let her go. I kind of felt bad, though. She did pick up and move here from Atlanta and now she already lost her job. I know it's not my responsibility, but I still wanted to see if I could find her something else. Kyle needed a new waitress and Leena would be great at that job. I had to beg him to hire her. Of course, he said yes. Neither Leena nor Jax seemed upset when I fired her. In fact, they both seemed happy about the job at KC's. I had a weird feeling that something wasn't right, I just couldn't figure out what.

Everywhere I go, Jax's eyes seemed to follow. He has been getting a little pushy lately. Maybe now, with the engagement, he will finally get the hint. I walk over to where Kyle and the rest of the guys from the band are getting ready to go up and play. I love watching him sing, not just because of how sexy he is on stage, but you can see how much he loves doing it. I walk up to him and smile as I lean up on my tiptoes to kiss his lips.

"What was that for?" he asks with a smile

"Just 'cause I love you," I say as I let him go, smacking him on the ass as he walks away.

Before they start playing, Kyle speaks," I want to thank you all for coming today to celebrate our engagement with us. You are more than just friends to us; you're our family. I have loved Amber my whole life, and she has made me so happy by agreeing to be my wife." If he keeps this up, I'm going to start crying. "I also want to thank Holly for doing such a great job planning this party, even though I was a pain in the ass most of the time." Everyone laughs. "So ... enough of me talking. I would like to dedicate our first song to my future wife; it's called *The Reason,* originally performed by Hoobastank." He smiles at me as the song begins.

He looks in my eyes through the whole song and tears are streaming down my face. I love this man so much more than I thought possible. I mouth, "I love you," when they finish the song. When the next one starts, Jax comes and sits down at my table.

"Are you okay? Why do you look so sad?" Jax asks, putting his hand over mine on the table. I quickly pull mine away.

"I'm fine, I'm not sad at all. Quite the opposite actually, they are happy tears. I have never been happier than I am with Kyle," I say as I look at Kyle and smile. I can tell he isn't pleased with Jax's close proximity to me.

"You know he is going to screw this up and end up hurting you again. Guys like him don't change, some girl is going to come along and he won't be able to resist the temptation. I care about you too much to stand by and watch him hurt you again." He is getting angry, but so am I. He doesn't know what he is talking about. Kyle would never cheat on me. I may not have known it six years ago, but I do know it now.

"Jax this has to stop. Kyle would never do anything to hurt me. Even if he did, I am not your responsibility to look after. Sorry to be blunt, but even if Kyle isn't in the picture, I don't have any romantic feelings for you. I never have, never will. I think it's time you finally realize there is nothing to wait around for." I start to feel bad for being so harsh because he looks like I kicked him in the nuts. Soon as he opens his mouth, I don't feel bad any longer.

"I know you think you don't love me, but it's only because he is blinding you to me. Once he isn't around, you'll see how much you love me and that we belong together." With that, he gets up and leaves. He is making me a little nervous. I have never seen him act like this before. Bringing him here may have been a huge mistake.

Kyle

THAT ASSHOLE is seriously pushing his luck. Besides the fact that I know he wants Amber, there is something else about him that makes me really uneasy. I'm not the only one who has noticed either. Paul, Holly, and even Marty have said something about him. I am not sure how to approach the subject with Amber, though, without sounding like the jealous boyfriend. I can tell whatever they are talking about right now has them both angry. I am just worried that I don't know what this guy is truly capable of. As soon as I see him storm off, I feel a little better knowing I don't have to worry about him … at least for tonight. I smile down at Amber. I hope he didn't upset her. Tonight is her night and she should be having fun.

Just as we are starting the next song, I hear a loud explosion. It sounds like it came from out front. I tell everyone to stay where they are. Paul and I try to find the source. Before I get to the front of the house, I can smell the smoke. As soon as I come around the corner, I see my truck engulfed in flames. Paul is calling 9-1-1 before it even registers with me what is really happening. How the hell could this happen? This is so surreal. I have no idea how to react. I glance over at Paul. The disbelief and shock on his face mirrors my own.

"The fire department and sheriff are on the way," Paul says as he puts his hand on my shoulder.

"Who the hell would do this to me?"

"I know three people off the top of my head. Beau, Darcie, or Jax," Paul says.

"Why would Jax do something like this?" Amber asks from behind us. She sounds frightened. I don't blame her. The fact that someone could do this scares the shit out of me too. I didn't hear her walk up. I don't know what to say to her. Those are the only three people that would come to my mind, too.

"Amber, I know Jax is your friend, and I could be wrong, but some of us are getting a really weird vibe from the guy. There is just something off about him. You should have a talk with Holly. She is getting the same feeling and she has firsthand experience with obsessive men," Paul says to her. I am expecting her to start defending him and yelling at the two of us, but she shocks us both.

"I am starting to wonder about him myself lately. He's changed since he has been here. I'm still not sure if this is something he is capable of, though," she says as she nuzzles up close to me.

"We aren't saying he did. He's just one of the three main possibilities. I am going to let everyone know what's going on," Paul says before walking out to the backyard.

"Promise me you will be careful around Jax. I am starting to get a little worried," I tell Amber as I kiss her forehead.

"I promise I will," she says.

Once the fire department arrived it didn't take too long to put the fire out. After investigating, they explain that this was definitely arson. The sheriff takes statements from everyone at the party. Paul and I both tell them the only three people we think it can be and why. I know Amber doesn't want to believe that Jax could do something like this, but I'm really not so sure.

CHAPTER
Fourteen

Amber

 IT WAS so late last night after everyone finally left. I decided to come into work a little later this morning. If I am being honest, I think some of it has to do with Jax. I'm a little nervous to see him today. I'm still not sure he is the one who set Kyle's truck on fire. I know he's been acting strange lately, but this just doesn't seem like something he would do.

Kyle comes up behind me and wraps his arms around me. He watches me in the mirror as I am finishing up my make-up. Even the littlest touches from him send sparks through my body and make me want to crawl right back into bed with him.

"How about I go into the center with you today, Princess?" he asks while placing kisses along my neck.

"Sweetie, you can't follow me everywhere I go."

"I know. I just wouldn't be able to stand it if anything ever happened to you."

I turn around in his arms and place my arms around his neck. He leans down to kiss me. I love kissing him. It's like everything around us disappears. I reluctantly break away from his lips.

"I love you."

"I love you, too"

"You have nothing to worry about. I'm never alone at the center, so if Jax does anything that makes me nervous, I will let someone know. Okay?" I smile up at him.

"Okay. But I am coming in at two to bring you lunch." He kisses me on the forehead and lets me get back to getting ready.

It is about nine o'clock when I pull into the center. Jax's car is parked in his spot. As I walk through the center to the stairs, I see Jax out back with a group of preschoolers. I go to put my purse away in my office. On my way back down, I see that Angel is here for the music classes today. I decide walk over to say hi before the kids come in. Shocked doesn't even begin to describe how I felt the first time he asked me if he could volunteer to do music classes. I was even more surprised when I asked him what ages he was comfortable with and he told me all ages. He just never struck me as a kid person. Just goes to show that looks can be deceiving. He comes off as your typical badass rocker. He is always hanging out with a different girl or several different girls, but he is great with the kids and they really love him.

"Morning, Angel."

"Well hello there, beautiful. How ya doing today?"

"Pretty good, busy as usual and the school kids haven't even gotten here yet."

"No problems with Jax this morning?"

"Nope, I haven't even seen him yet." All of the little four and five year olds start to walk into the room. "I'll let you get started. I just wanted to say hi," I say as I start to walk out. He grabs my arm and gets closer so no one else can hear him.

"Amber, if you have any problems, let me know. Even if you just have an odd feeling, okay?" He looks so serious. Did everyone get a bad vibe from Jax? If so, why was I the only one who didn't see it?

"I will. Thank you." I give him a kiss on the cheek which makes all the kids giggle and Angel blush.

I head back to my office and tackle the pile of paperwork that waits on my desk. I am so engrossed in what I am doing, the knock on my door startles me. I glance at the clock to see what time it is. It was only one o'clock. Too early to be Kyle.

"Come in!" I yell. Darcie walks through my door. Just what I don't need is a dose of her. I am not in the mood for her bullshit today. She has her usual shit-eating grin on her face as she waltzes right in and sits in the chair across from me.

"What can I do for you, Darcie?"

"How was your party last night? I heard it ended with a big bang." She laughs.

"You bitch!" I stand up and bolt around my desk ready to yank her out of her chair. Before I can get to her, she stands up and pulls a gun out of her purse. All of the anger is gone, instantly replaced with ice cold fear. I slip back in my chair. I knew she has a few screws loose, but I didn't see something like this coming. What the hell is she going to do? Shoot me here, in my office? If so, she'll never get out of the building before someone gets to her.

"You are going to quietly come with me. I swear to God, Amber, if you try to tip anyone off or get away from me, I will shoot the first kid I see." Her voice is deathly serious as she creeps closer to me. "Do you understand?"

"Yes," I comply.

"Good. Now, grab your purse, leave your cell phone on your desk, and let's go." I do as she asks. I don't want any of the children to get hurt. I walk along with her following me and try to look as normal as possible. I smile as I pass the kids and their counselors. As we walk out of the front doors, Darcie leads me to her car and tells me to get in the driver's side.

"Where are you taking me?" I ask as I start her car.

"You are going to be so surprised," she says with an eerie laugh.

"Do you really think by killing me, Kyle will be with you?" I know I shouldn't poke the bear, but I think I'm still in shock.

"Anything is possible. I'm going to be there to help him pick up the pieces of his broken heart when you leave him again. Most of all, you are my ticket to finally being free."

What the hell is that supposed to mean? Free from what? I don't have time to ask, she directs me to drive a couple miles until there is nothing around and tells me to pull over. This is it I thought to myself, she took me here to shoot me. Darcie tells me to get in the back seat. Before I can figure out what she is doing, she puts a cloth over my face, and everything is black.

My eye lids are heavy. I try so hard to open them, but they just won't cooperate. I hear voices off in a distance, but I can't tell who they are. I try moving my arms, hoping I'll be able to feel something, anything, that tells me where I am, but they are tied tightly. My heart is thudding in my chest, I can feel the blood rushing in my ears, and a cold sweat breaks out over my skin. Terror and panic consume me. I try to calm my breathing, deep, steady breaths, and concentrate on opening my eyes. When my eyes finally open, everything is blurry, unfocused. I blink several times, trying to adjust. As soon as they come into focus, I look around, taking in my surroundings. I am bound by my wrists and ankles to a bed. I look around the small bedroom. The walls are painted white and lack any paintings or decor. There is one small window that allows light to filter in. I can see it is nailed shut. The hardwood floors are scratched and worn. A small dresser is the only piece of furniture in the room. The place reminds me of some of the fishing cabins we visited when I was younger.

I hear footsteps coming closer. The door opens and Darcie walks in with Beau trailing behind her.

"What the fuck is going on?" I yell. Beau sits next to me on the bed. I try to move away, but can't. He starts running his hand through my hair and my stomach rolls, the bile rising in my throat.

"Calm down, darlin'. You and I never had a chance to get to know each other all those years ago thanks to that asshole Kyle. Well, now we will. I got Darcie here to help me. In return, she gets her freedom from me and her shot at Kyle. Everyone is happy."

"You both are sick! I want nothing to do with you, and Kyle will never want her!" I turn my head so I don't have to look at him

"Don't be that way. We had something back in school. I know you liked me." He grips my chin in his hand and forcefully turns my face back to him.

"I *never* liked you like that. The thought of being with you makes my stomach turn," I say and spit in his face. A sharp pain radiates through my head as his fist connects with the side of my face. I can taste the blood in my mouth. Shit … that hurt.

"I don't like doing that to you, darlin'. You are going to have to learn to be nice. I know you will love me. It may just take a little while for you to come around. It's a good thing I'm a patient man. I will punish you if I have to, though. Won't I Darcie?"

He turns my head to face her and I can see the fear in her eyes. "She can tell you. If you don't behave, you will be disciplined. I do not tolerate bad behavior." He gets so close to my face, I feel his hot breath on my skin, the putrid smell invading my nostrils. I gag and force myself to swallow the bile that rises further. It takes everything in me to be still and keep my mouth shut. "Don't worry I am going to let you get good and rested before all of the fun starts." He leans back down and kisses my cheek and I control the urge to head-butt the son of a bitch. As soon as the two of them are out the door and it closes behind them, I let the tears flow. I have no idea where I am. How is anyone going to find me? I would rather Beau kill me before he lays one filthy hand on me. The last thing I think about before falling asleep is how happy I've been these last few months with Kyle.

Kyle

I TRY calling Amber to see what she wants for lunch, but she doesn't answer. Normally it wouldn't be a big deal. After last night, though, I am a little on edge. I push the thought away, she's probably just busy and left her phone in her office. I decide to drive a little out of the way to get her favorite grilled scallops to surprise her. I pull into the youth center and see her and Jax's cars parked in their spots. I park my rental car and head inside. I see Angel in one of the music rooms with a group of little kids. I never would have pegged him for a kid friendly kind of guy. I wave to him on my way upstairs to Amber's office.

I knock on her office door. When I don't hear anything, I check to see if it's locked. It's not, so I open the door to find it empty. I put the bag of food on her desk. I check Jax's office, his door is open, and no one is in there either. I go back down the stairs, heading to see if she's downstairs or outside. Angel walks out of the room he was working in.

"Hey. Have you seen Amber?"

"I saw her when she came in this morning. She wasn't in her office?"

"No and she knew I was coming at two o'clock."

"I'll look around in here, why don't you check outside." He gives me a reassuring look.

He knows I'm on edge after last night and I appreciate him not calling me out on probably overreacting. I walk down the hallway to the back doors. When I get outside, I see Jax and another counselor with a couple groups of kids. As much as I don't want to, I need to find out if he has seen Amber today. He notices me and starts walking my way.

"Hey, Jax. Have you seen Amber today?"

"No, I haven't. I have been out here all day. Is something wrong?"

Before I could answer, Angel comes barreling out of the back doors. By the look on his face, he hasn't found her either. This feeling that something is terribly wrong slams into me like a freight train.

"What is it?" I ask not knowing if I really want Angel to answer me.

"One of the counselors saw her leaving with a woman a little after one o'clock. But nobody knows who she was."

"Follow me. We can check security footage from today. I had Amber install cameras everywhere," Jax says as he starts running back inside with Angel and I following close behind.

Who would she leave with and why? I clench my jaw, clenching and unclenching my hands. My anxiety level spikes and that feeling twists my stomach into knots. I do not have a good feeling about this at all. When we get to Jax's office, he pulls all the video feeds up on his computer. He waves me around his desk so I can see what he sees. We see Darcie come into her office. What the hell is she doing here? Amber stands up quickly and her body stiffens. She looks terrified. Then, I see it. I can feel the blood drain from my face and my hands start to shake. In fear or anger, I'm not sure. She has a fucking gun pointed at Amber. I can't move. I barely register that Jax on the phone calling the sheriff and Angel calling Paul. My stomach does a painful flip-flop and I quickly run out of the office to the bathroom. I barely make it to the toilet before I start heaving. Once I know I have nothing left in my stomach, I start running down the stairs and bolt toward the front door. Suddenly, two sets of arms grab ahold of me, yanking me to a stop.

"What the Fuu …" I turn and see Paul and Marcus have a pretty tight grip on me.

"And where do you think you are going?" Paul asks with a raised eyebrow.

"Where do you think? I can't just sit here and do nothing. I have to go find her." I try breaking free from them, but it's no use. My whole goddamned world has just tipped upside down and these assholes are keeping me from fixing it. Not that I know where she is or how to fix it. I can't just do nothing.

"We need to wait for the sheriff to get here. We can't go halfcocked and make things worse." I nod. I know he is right, but I feel so damn helpless. My girl is in trouble and I'm going to sit here on my ass doing nothing. Some fucking man I am. This is all my fault. I should've been keeping her safe not putting her in danger because I screwed a crazy bitch. We all walk back upstairs to wait for the sheriff. I sit in a chair in the corner of the conference room. Jax has a laptop set up to show the sheriff the video footage. When he finishes, he walks over to me.

"If I can do anything to help, man, please let me know." I look up at him. He tries to smile, but he can't do it any more than I can right now. I can tell he is being sincere and wants to help.

"Thanks. If you could just make sure everything keeps running as it should, that would be great. I know Amber will appreciate that. I will make sure to keep you filled in on anything we find out."

Sheriff Lee Beasley walks in and he looks about as upset as the rest of us. He has known Amber and me since we were little. Even though he was about twenty years younger than Amber's grandfather, they were pretty good friends. Jax goes through the video with him and I can see him cringe when the gun comes into view. I can see the anger in his face when he recognizes Darcie on the screen.

"You boys know if we are dealing with Beau Hartly, we have a problem, right?" I look at him, confused. I am not sure what he is trying to say.

Before I can ask, he continues, "We have responded to some pretty nasty domestic calls over the years between him and Darcie. Of course, she didn't follow through with pressing charges, out of fear I suppose. There have been three women over the last six years disappear. We have always thought it was Beau, but never had enough proof to charge him." He gives me a sad look. "We have found two of the three bodies over the last couple years." At this, I totally break down. The tears leak out on their own accord and I feel the fury pumping through my veins, the adrenaline coursing through me. I can't control it. We have to find her. So help me God if that son of a bitch has harmed a single fucking hair on her head. I will fucking kill him with my own bare hands.

CHAPTER
Fifteen

Amber

M**Y HEAD** is throbbing. Every time I take a breath, a stabbing pain shakes me. Last night I convinced Beau to untie me so I could go to the bathroom. I promised I would behave. As soon as he untied me I tried to run. He and Darcie caught me before I got to the front door. By the time Beau finished with me, I really wished I hadn't done that. He punched me right in the face, knocking me to the floor. Then, his boot connected hard with my ribs. I saw him rear back, ready to kick me again. I tried to cover my stomach with my arms, but his boot flashed before my eyes. Now, I have splitting, seriously splitting headache, but I can move. Only one hand is tied to the bed. I try to turn and stretch, but I hurt all over. I lift my hand to my face, feeling how swollen my bottom lip is.

Footsteps are coming toward the room. My pulse speeds up and my whole body tenses. I never pictured him as an evil man. To being capable of this. The door opens slowly and Darcie walks in with a tray of food. My stomach growls, but my mind heaves at this response. She walks over to the other side of the bed and sets the tray down.

"Are you hungry? I made you a sandwich," she says as she gives me a slight smile. "Amber, you need to eat. I can hear your stomach from here." She's right. I am starving; it's been over twenty-four hours since I've eaten. Against my minds refusal, I pick up the sandwich and take a bite. It's either the best damn turkey sandwich I have ever had or I was really starving. I give her a small smile. "I really am sorry I had to bring you here. Beau promised if I did it he would leave me alone for good. It doesn't look like that is going to happen, though." She looks sad and broken. There are cuts and bruises on her face. I refuse to feel sorry for her.

"You can't honestly be trying to make me feel sorry for you?"

"No, but you need to realize I have been living with his torture for over seven very long years. Think about the lengths you would go to get away from him after one day. Now, imagine seven years of what you have experienced, plus much worse. I am not making excuses. I hate what I did and I'm sorry. But, I was desperate. I thought he was going to finally free me. He has, since then, made it perfectly clear to me that it's never going to happen," she states, her voice wobbly with emotion. It was then that starts crying. Deep, heaving sobs that wrench me. Damn it! I'm too soft hearted. How do I know she isn't making all of this up?

"Then, let's help each other get the hell out of here."

"There is no way out! We are at Beau's fishing cabin. The only way in and out is by boat. We are in the middle of the Everglades with nothing but swamp and gators for miles. He didn't even take my phone. There's no chance of reception out here." My stomach rolls at her words.

"He's done this before, Amber."

"Done what?"

"I'm so sorry, Amber, for doing this to you," she says between sobs.

As I lay here, seemingly helpless, I take in her words. I'm confused, but I'm patient. And strong. I fight back my compassion and appear irritated, waiting for her to continue. She's not the one tied up, she wasn't bound and kidnapped. I let my anger stir, still patiently.

"He has taken women and held them out here until he had his fill of them. Then, he killed them. We aren't getting out of here alive," she finally admits. I still at her words, yet I'm not surprised. I dig deep into myself and find my hope. Kyle.

"Kyle will look for me. They will find us. We can't give up Darcie." I don't think she buys it, not that I can blame her. I don't really believe it myself at this point, either. But, I try. It shouldn't surprise me. I'm finally happy, truly happy, have everything I could possibly want, and it's all going to end.

"How are they going to even know where to look? They won't know I took you."

"Yes, they will. Jax had security cameras installed at the youth center in every room. They will come look for us." I try to look confident, but I'm praying they find us in time. I know, deep down, Kyle won't give up until he finds us.

I hear Beau coming down the hallway. Darcie must have heard him, too, because her whole body tenses up. She is terrified of him. It's written all over her face. She gets up and starts to clean up the lunch tray. He opens the door and looks between the both of us.

"What are you ladies up to in here?" he asks maliciously. "Take that stuff out of here and close the door on your way out, Darcie." He gives her a stern look. She gives me a sympathetic look, quickly picks up the tray, and hurries out of the room. As soon as the door closes, he slowly makes his way closer to the bed and sits down next to me. I inch over as much as my restraints allow. He leans in close to me and runs his hand along my swollen lips.

"You need to learn to do as I say and be nicer to me. I won't have to do things like this to you if you're a good girl. I've been in love with you since we were kids. I have waited a very long time to be with you. I don't take pleasure in hurting you." He runs his hand along my cheek and my skin crawls. He is definitely a few sandwiches short of a picnic.

"Eventually, you will love me. You'll see. We both know Kyle will end up hurting you anyway. It is just a matter of time." Oh yes, this man is seriously delusional. Darcie's right. We are never getting out of here alive. Beau leans down even further. Before I realize what he's doing, his lips are on mine. I try to move my head away, but he grips my face with both of his large hands. When I feel his tongue slide across my lips, I feel physically sick. I bite down on his lip, hard. The taste of blood fills my mouth.

"You BITCH!" he roars as his fist connects with the side of my face so hard my ear rings. I scream from the pain. Beau is standing up now and pacing around the room. I can tell he is fuming, trying to rein in his temper. I pray he is going to be successful. He sits on the edge of the bed again.

"Why do you force me to lash out at you this way? I only want to love you. I don't want to punish you, but you keep doing these things that leave me no choice. Why?" he asks. I should be smart and just tell him what he wants to hear. Normally, I am not one to rock the boat. He just pisses me off to no end. The fact that I am scared shitless really doesn't help either. So, here I go, opening my mouth again knowing I should just shut up.

"Why? Are you seriously asking me that? For one, you can't make someone love you. I am sorry, Beau, but I have just never felt that way for you. No matter what you do, that will not change. And two, you sent your ex-wife to take me at gunpoint. That did not win you any points. And three, the worst of them all, you laid your hands on me. Even if I did love you, the first time you hit me I would have let you go. That is not something you do to someone you claim to love." I look him straight in the eye, waiting for the blows to come. What he said and did next not only shocked me but made me sick at the same time.

"You know, you're right. I should not have hit you. From now on, instead of punishing you, I am going to punish Darcie. Just know, you have really pissed me off." I can't let him do this. I don't like the girl, but I don't wish her harm because of me. I can't believe I am going to beg him to hit me.

"No, please don't do that. She didn't do anything."

"No. You were right. I love you, and I shouldn't hit you, but I sure as hell don't love her anymore. And like I told you before, I don't get any real pleasure when I hurt you, but that doesn't mean I don't get pleasure from hurting other women." He laughs, bends down to kiss my cheek, then walks out the door. A few minutes later, I hear the crash of dishes on the floor and Darcie's screams. I cover my head with the pillow and pray that someone will find us.

Kyle

I ALWAYS knew Beau was a little unstable, but I never pictured him as a fucking serial killer. God, I hope Amber is okay. I have driven all over the place looking for any signs of them. Who knows if they are still even in the state? Now, I'm sitting on a damn bar stool. Driving or sitting on the bar stool, that has been my life for the last twenty-four hours. Paul, Marcus, and Angel are watching me like a hawk. Guess they are either waiting for me to go off halfcocked or break down. Hell, I would go if I knew where the son of a bitch is. As for breaking down, I'm just not there yet. Holly has been mothering me. I love her for it, but I just want to be left alone unless someone has info on my girl.

All of this waiting is driving me insane. I feel helpless just sitting here and not doing anything, but what else can I do? We have no idea where else to look. They are looking for both Darcie's car and Beau's truck. They have someone watching their house, the diner where Darcie works, and the construction company that Beau works at. So far, no luck. There are all kinds of hiding places in this area. Some of those places you can't get to by car, foot, or even an old boat. You need an airboat. Sheriff Beasley sits down on the stool next to me. He gives me a sly smile as he pats me on the shoulder. He's not in his uniform, but his gun is still very visible. This pisses me off. He should be working around the clock looking for Amber. He must be able to read the look on my face, because I can tell he knows exactly what I am thinking.

"Before you get all worked up, boy, hear me out. I am not in uniform because a little birdy told me those no good buddies of Beau's are coming in here for a beer after work. I haven't been able to get any information out of them in my official sheriff capacity up to this point. So, I figured we could try an unofficial tactic here in your bar with a little help from Paul and Angel." By the wicked grin on his face I know exactly what he has in mind. "I figure you are pretty tired of waiting around for news. So, ya ready to get your hands a little dirty?"

"Paul, can you go make sure no one is in the pool room, then close the doors. We are going to need it in a little bit," I ask.

Paul smiles at me then the sheriff and takes care of the pool room. Sheriff Beasley smiles at me knowing I am more than ready to get my hands dirty, and so are the boys. Angel slides up on the stool next to me with a grin from ear to ear. Angel is always up for a fight. Not to mention he has been beating himself up since Amber disappeared. He feels guilty because he was there that day and didn't notice Darcie take her. I don't blame him at all; he couldn't have known, especially when he had a room full of kids to tend to.

The front doors to the bar open and in walk Beau's two sidekicks. Hell, I don't even know their names. Sheriff Beasley isn't wasting any time. He tells Paul and Angel to go grab the boys and get them in the back. Paul and Angel are all over them in seconds. The boys don't stand a chance. Paul and Angel are like hulks compared to these two. The size difference is actually comical. As we are following them to the back, Sheriff Beasley informs me that the bozo's names are Rick and Andy. Not that I really care what the hell their names are, but I figure it would better to call them by their real names rather than bozo one and bozo two. As soon as I close the door behind me, Beasley is in Rick's face with his fist twisted in the collar of his shirt so tight the boy is struggling for air.

"What the hell, Sheriff?" Rick spat.

"Today, I'm just plain Beasley. That is an unfortunate thing for the two of you." He shoves Rick so hard into the chair I think it's going to flip over. I have to control my laughter. I had forgotten what a badass Beasley can be when the need arises. Thank God I've never been on his bad side. He isn't overly muscular, but you can tell he is a strong man, even for his age. He looks pretty damn intimidating when he wants to even though he is about thirty years older than the rest of us.

"You boys have not wanted to help me find Beau. I have only asked for any information regarding a place he could be hiding and I know you boys have such information. Let me also remind you, he is wanted for questioning in three murders and now the kidnapping of his wife and Amber Lewis. I have known Amber since she was a baby, and her granddaddy was my best friend, so this is very personal for me. But, I am also the sheriff so I have a line I can't cross. These guys, however, don't," he says as he looks between the three of us. "Now ... these two here, they love Amber like a sister," Beasley states as he points to Angel and Paul. They both glare at the two scared men sitting in front of them. "They are also the best friends of this man who has been madly in love with Amber since he was in diapers. Which means they will do anything to help him get her back. And I do mean *anything*. Now, I am going to leave the room so that I do not cross any of those lines and let you boys chat."

He turns and faces us, gives us a wink, and walks out to the bar. Yeah, Beasley was never paying for anything in this place again. Paul and Angel start moving forward, closer to Rick and Andy. I am taller than Angel and the same height as Paul, but to have both of them after me would scare me shitless, so I can just imagine what is going through the heads of these little assholes. I am not surprised to see the two boys looking at each other, trying to decide what they should do. As soon as I see Paul's hand tighten into a fist, Andy, the smaller of the two, starts talking.

"Okay, man, he has a cabin out in the glades. The only way to get to it is by airboat. I swear, we haven't seen or heard from him in days. I have no idea if that is where he is at or not." They explain to us exactly how to get to this cabin. Beasley gets on the phone right away, trying to get us an airboat. They know Beau is an asshole, but like the rest of us, they had no idea what he was really capable of. I never realized how badly he was infatuated with Amber. Beasley quickly announces that he has found us an airboat. God, please let her be okay.

CHAPTER
Sixteen

Amber

AFTER WHAT felt like forever, I hear the noise from the kitchen quiet. No matter how tight I held the pillow to my head, it didn't drown out Darcie's cries, or the loud blows from Beau. I feel sick to my stomach. I should have just kept my damn mouth shut and taken whatever he was going to do to me. I may have saved my own ass, but I ended up sending him right after Darcie instead. I feel so guilty. He has got to be crazy if he thinks I am ever going to willingly love him. I will end up dying in this hell before that ever happens.

I can hear Beau's loud footsteps coming down the hall. There is also a constant rasp on the floor, like he's dragging something behind him. Darcie. Please God, let her be okay. The door opens and he drags her across the floor to the other side of the bed. He roughly picks her up and puts her next to me on the bed. I look over at her and wince. It takes everything I have in me not to lash out at the monster standing over her. Keep calm. Bide my time. How could someone do that to another human being? There is so much blood on her face, it's hard to tell exactly where it's coming from. Under the blood, her face is swollen and her arms are painted in bruises. Her chest is steadily rising and falling, but she is unconscious.

"Beau, you can't just leave her like this." I give him a pleading look. He had to have loved her at some point to have married her, right?

"I can and will. I'm not wasting any more time on this bitch."

"Please, Beau, I will clean her up and take care of the cuts if you will get me a first aid kit, some water, and a wash cloth."

"I suppose you expect me to untie you, too. Why do you give a fuck about what happens to her anyway?" he spat as he got closer to me. I am starting to get nervous. The last thing I want to do right now is piss him off again. Although, it doesn't seem to take a whole lot to get his temper to flare. I look him in the eyes, pleading with mine, trying to show him that I'm not trying to pull anything, that I truly only want to help Darcie.

"I will let you play nurse for a while. But, Amber, you and I are going to get acquainted later on." He gets right in front of my face, so close that I can feel his breath. "If you can't play nice this time, there won't be any way to talk me into walking away." With that, he walks out. A few minutes later, he comes back in with a first aid kit, a pot of water, and some towels. He releases my arm and reminds me to behave. After he closes the door, I hear it lock from the outside.

The second I move, my ribs scream in protest. I almost forgot about my own beatings at Beau's hands. But, compared to Darcie's, mine were nothing. I slowly sit up and slide my legs over to the floor, a wave of dizziness sweeping over me. I look to my own cuts and bruises, deciding to care for them after. I slowly ease off the bed and walk to the other side where I can reach her better. I quickly start looking over her face. There is a bad cut above her eyebrow that probably needs stitches. Hopefully there is something in the first aid kit that would do for now. I clean everything with water first. Jesus, she's a mess. He beat her worse than I thought. As I am wiping the large cut with an alcohol wipe, Darcie starts coming to. I put a butterfly bandage on the cut, and it seems to close it up. Darcie looks up and gives me a small smile.

"Thanks, Amber. Why are you being so nice to me? I really don't deserve your kindness ... not after the things I have done to you." By the way she is gasping and pausing in between the words, I can tell it hurts her to breathe. She probably has some bruised ribs, possibly broken.

"It's my fault he did this to you. I am so sorry," I say as guilt washes over me again. If I wouldn't have tried to get Beau to leave me alone, he never would have gone after her in the first place.

"I am the one who should be apologizing. You wouldn't be here if I would have had the guts to leave him when I had the chance. I just felt hopeless, like no matter where I went he would find me. I never should have let him talk me into bringing you here. I hope someday you will be able to forgive me. I'm really not a bad person, I promise," she says as she starts to cry.

I sit next to her and wrap my arm around her. I can sympathize with her. I haven't been through as much for as long as she has, but I have felt pretty damn hopeless in the last twenty-four hours. As I sit here, trying to comfort her, I start to think Darcie is right. We are never getting out of here. I thought Kyle would have found us by now and Beau isn't going to leave me alone forever. Neither one of us is in any shape to try to overpower him, especially when he has a gun somewhere. We just need to hang on for as long as we possibly can without pissing him off. Hopefully that will save both of us another beating.

We must have fallen asleep. When I open my eyes, I notice that it's getting dark outside. My stomach starts growling so loudly it wakes Darcie up. She looks over and laughs which makes me laugh. And, it feels good. After everything we've been through, are still going through, it gives me hope and the strength I need to survive this.

Unfortunately, I hear the all too familiar footsteps walking down the hallway. I can feel Darcie's body start to tremble as dread consumes me. I don't know what the hell he plans on doing next and I really don't want to find out. I just want to run as far away from here as I can.

Darcie reaches over and grips my hand tightly. We both jump when we hear the click of the latch being unlocked. Beau walks in slowly, looking between the two of us and shaking his head.

"Are you two bonding or some shit now?" he scoffs. "I hate to break up the girl time y'all have going, but I am going to need some alone time with Amber, so you are going to need to wait for me in the other room, Darcie," he says, never taking his eyes off me. My stomach starts rolling, nausea settling in. The last thing I want is to be alone with him.

"No," Darcie says so quietly I almost don't hear her. She squeezes my hand tighter as soon as the words leave her mouth. Beau looks at her in disbelief and moves around the bed until he is next to her.

"I don't think I heard you, Darcie. Let's try this again. I said, go and wait for me in the other room. Now!" he says sharply. The look on his face dares her to mess with him. I look at Darcie, her face set with determination. Normally, I would say "go girl" and high five her, but now is not the time.

"You heard me. I said NO. I am not leaving Amber alone with you." She is looking him straight in the eyes. For a second, it looks like Beau is going to back down. The corners of his lips twitch like he is smiling. I should have known better. He's not the type of guy to back down. Before I realize what is happening, he has her by the neck and is picking her up off the bed. She is still clinging onto my hand for dear life, but he is pulling her so hard that I am getting closer to the edge of the bed. She is gasping for air because he is squeezing her throat so hard. Once he gets her off the bed, he holds her up so her feet are barely touching the floor and hurls her against the wall with so much force, it jerks me right off the bed and I land with a thud on the hard wood floor face first. SHIT! That hurts. Beau kicks me out of his way and stomps over to Darcie. I have to do something. Blood is steadily flowing out of my nose and I can feel my cheeks starting to swell, but I latch onto any amount of adrenaline I have and pull myself up. I launch forward, jumping in front of Darcie before Beau can get to her.

"What are you doing?" Darcie whispers to me.

"We are in this together."

Beau is livid. His nostrils flare, his eyes get hard, his jaw clenches, and his breathing picks up. He hates that I took the control away from him. Hates that I dismissed him so boldly. Hates that I am standing up to him. Above all, hates the fact that the two of us are standing up for each other. It's much easier for him to control us when he could keep us apart.

"I have had enough of the two of you," he growls as he pulls a gun from the waistband of his jeans. "You," he points to me, "get the fuck back on the bed now!" I'm torn. I really don't want to get shot, but I don't want to leave Darcie alone either. Before I have a chance to decide, we all hear something. It sounds like an airboat. Hope blooms once more in my belly. Oh, please, let that be someone here to help us.

"Both of you be quiet. If either of you make a sound, I will shoot you both. I am done playing games." He quickly leaves the room and locks the door. Darcie and I huddle together and slide to the floor in the corner, praying we are about to get out of here.

Kyle

BEASLEY DOESN'T want a huge group of people and several roaring airboats to tip Beau off to our arrival, so it is only Paul, Angel, Beasley, and me. It's enough people to overpower without freaking his ass out with a shit load of cops coming at him. However, Beasley has the sheriff's helicopter with backup and a medical helicopter on standby if we need them. We were all given sheriff-issued Kevlar vests, but hopefully they won't be tested.

Beasley is the only one armed. With good reason. At this point, I would shoot Beau just for the hell of it. I hated him before. Now, there isn't a word strong enough to describe what I feel for him. The plan is for Beasley and me to contain Beau. Paul and Angel are supposed to find Amber and Darcie.

We still have no clue what role Darcie is playing in all of this. We know she is the one who initially took Amber, but with everything we have learned about Beau, he could have forced her to do it.

The boat ride to the cabin only took us about twenty-five minutes, although it felt like two days. I just held onto the hope that they were here and Amber was okay. I honestly don't know what I would do without her. Especially when I didn't force her protection a much as I should have. I love that woman more than life. She is my life. My everything. I cannot get her back just to lose her all over again. I don't ever want to know what life is like without her again. I lived through it once and I damn sure wouldn't do it again.

Thank God for the guys. I couldn't ask for better friends. These past days, I don't know what I would've done without them. Not many people would be willing to put themselves into harm's way for someone else. Goes to show that I'm not the only one who has had their heart stolen by Amber.

As soon as the cabin comes into view, hope swells in my chest. There are lights on inside. That has to be a good sign. I try not to let it overwhelm me. Someone is here, I tell myself. It doesn't mean Amber is here. An airboat rests at the dock … another sign of life. Beasley cuts the engine a little ways away from the cabin so we can go in quietly. I feel my body tense as hope turns to fear. There is no way of knowing what we are going to find once we walk through that front door.

We get the boat docked and make our way to the cabin door. Beasley motions for us to stand back while he tests the door knob. It gives. Not locked. He slowly turns the knob, pushes the door open, and steps in with his gun ready. My heart is thuds I my chest, beating so fast and hard I can feel it in my ears. The cabin is small. You can easily see the entire space, including two doors toward the back. Bedrooms? Beasley pauses, tearing my concentration from the doors I hope Amber is behind. He motions with one hand toward the back door. Through the kitchen, we see that it is open. He wastes no time.

"Check the bedrooms for the girls!" he shouts as he runs out the backdoor.

The three of us tread lightly down the hallway. The first door is open and we can see that it is empty. For a second, my stomach drops. I remind myself there is still one more. When we get to that door, it is latched with a padlock. She has to be in there. Now, we just have to figure out how to get it opened.

"Amber, are you in there, Princess?" I yell through the door. I'm holding my breath, praying I get an answer. When I finally do, I fall to my knees. It is the absolute sweetest sound I have ever heard.

"Kyle, is that you? We are in here!" she cries.

"We have to figure out how to get this lock off. Are either of you hurt?"

"A little, but I don't think it's too serious. Please, just hurry and get us out of here." She sounds so tired and shaken. Paul runs into the kitchen to see if there is anything in there we can use to get in the door. He comes back empty-handed. Beasley is behind him saying Beau took off. Shit! He must have the key. I hope they can find him before he gets too far away.

"Amber … you and Darcie stand as far away from the door as possible, and get on the ground," Beasley instructs her. Once she yells back that she is all set, he tells us all to get back. He stands back, fires a shot at each hinge, then walks up to it, kicking it. The door flies open, broken from its hinges, yet still connected by the lock. If I wasn't so anxious to get to Amber, it might have been kind of funny.

I run past Beasley into the room. I stop dead in my tracks the second I see Amber's face. Fuck! What did that bastard do to her? She has blood all over her clothes and face. There are bruises all over her face, including a huge black eye. If I ever get my hands on that son of a bitch, I am going to kill him. She stands up, and I can see it hurts her to do so. We need to get her to the hospital and get her examined. We meet each other in the middle of the room and I am almost scared to touch her. I don't want to hurt her. She must know that's what I am thinking because all of a sudden she crushes herself against me. So, I wrap her in my arms and hold her tight.

"You came. I knew you would find me," she cries.

"Always, Princess. I will always find you," I tell her as I gently hold her face in my hands to look it over. It feels so good to have her in my arms. Paul and Angel come over and kiss the top of her head, saying how glad they are that we found her. Angel grabs the first aid kit from the bed and brings it over to Darcie. She definitely got the worst of it. Amber must notice me looking.

"First, she was beat unconscious so that he would leave me alone. Then, he wanted her to leave the room so he could be alone with me. She stood up to him knowing what he would do to her." She has tears streaming down her face. "Kyle, I don't want her punished. She has been abused by him for years. None of this is her fault."

"I don't think that is up to us, but we will talk to Beasley." I kiss her forehead. Paul has brought in a wet towel and another first aid kit from the boat so we can clean Amber up. She sits on the bed and I kneel in front of her. I gently use the towel to clean all of the dried blood off her face. She tells me what has happened since Darcie took her from the center. Every time she tells me about Beau hurting her, I feel sick. And so pissed I want to hit something. Primarily Beau. She never should have gone through any of this shit. I take a deep breath to calm myself down and focus on getting her out of here and to a hospital.

"Let's get you two out of here and to the hospital to get checked out, okay?" I say as I put my hand out to help her up off the bed.

"I can't wait to get out of here," she says as she takes my hand and starts to walk in front of me.

"Oh … by the way, Princess, I love you. I have missed you like crazy," I tell her as I pull her in for a soft kiss so I don't hurt her cut and swollen lips. She is not going for the soft kiss, however. She starts kissing me like I am a bottle of ice-cold water in the middle of the desert. As soon as her tongue slides between my lips, I am lost to her. I miss her taste, her feel, and her sounds. Every ounce of love I felt for her I am trying to portray in this kiss. And of course, when she kisses me like that, the man in me pops out. I'm not being figurative. I am getting so fucking hard it hurts. Beasley is at the door, clearing his throat.

"Okay, you two. There's plenty of time for that later. Let's get the hell out of here," he says as we all make our way out to the boat. On the ride back I wonder if they are going to find Beau, and if not, will he just vanish, never to be heard from again? Are we going to be watching over our shoulders for the rest of our lives?

CHAPTER
Seventeen

Amber

WE GO straight to the hospital. By the time they are finishing all the tests, it's almost ten in the morning. Sheriff Beasley comes in and takes my statement so I don't have to go to the station and do it. For that, I am grateful. By the time we walk out of the hospital, it's one in the afternoon. Three days. Three days have passed. Three days I've been dealing with this shit. All things considered, physically I am pretty lucky. A couple bruised ribs and five stitches. What my mental state will be like after this is anyone's guess. I would feel a lot better if they had caught Beau. He doesn't seem like the type of guy that gives up very easily. I know Kyle is worried about Beau being out there, but he's not letting it show.

I haven't been able to stop holding onto Kyle. I feel like if I let him go, I will lose him forever. I didn't think I would ever see him again. The thought of never being with Kyle again frightened me more than knowing I was probably going to die. I just want to be home, snuggled up in his arms, safe and sound in our bed. Just thinking about it makes me smile. His deep, sexy voice breaks through my daydream.

"What are you thinking about that has you smiling so pretty over there?" he asks. He sounds more relaxed than he was a couple hours ago, which I am grateful for. We need to live in the moment, be happy that we have each other, and be grateful we are together. There are no guarantees that we will have anything past this moment, so why live in constant fear and worry about what might happen? I am not going to do it. I am going to enjoy every second I have with Kyle, our friends, and my center.

"I was thinking about getting you home and in our bed," I say seductively. Operation living in the moment commenced.

"I was thinking of running you a nice hot bubble bath. Then getting into it with you to keep you company. Once you are nice and relaxed and all clean, I will take you to bed and hold you tight in my arms until you fall asleep." He has a sheepish grin on his face.

"That actually sounds perfect." And it does. As long as Kyle is by my side, I'm happy with whatever we do. He is my soul mate, my other half. Over the past couple days, without Kyle in my life, I honestly don't think I would have the strength or willpower to pick myself up and keep going. There always seems to be some tragedy or heartache that follows me, but I can always pick myself up and keep going. This time is not going to be any different. Having Kyle by my side, makes me certain.

"We're home, Princess." I love the sound of that. We're home. Our home, together. I look over at him and smile. I can't help but smile when I look at him. He isn't just a handsome man, he is truly beautiful inside and out. He gets out of the truck, comes around to my side, and opens my door. I turn to get out, but he doesn't move away. He steps closer, positioning himself between my legs. He wraps his arms around my waist and pulls me closer to him. For a moment, we just stare into each other's eyes, no words needed. I can see the love he has for me and the fear he has felt thinking he might lose me. It is almost like looking into a mirror. When he finally starts to speak, his voice is filled with emotion.

"I love you so much. The last couple days, not knowing where you were or what was happening to you, just about killed me. Being without you is like being held under water. The longer you were gone, the less air I had. I would drown without you in my life." Every word he speaks fills my heart. They are the sweetest, most romantic words I have ever heard. The tears start to fall on their own accord. I can't help it. I just hope I don't look like a blubbering mess.

He wipes the tears away with his thumbs as he continues, "I know we said we were going to wait a while before we set a date to get married. I don't want to wait … not after what happened. Anything can happen at any time. Life is too fucking unpredictable. I don't know what is going to happen in the future, but I do know, more than anything I have ever wanted in my entire life, I want to be your husband." Wow. The words evade me as my tears pick up, almost turning into sobs. I breathe deep and gather my bearings. I look into his eyes. He's nervous, his eyes pleading.

"I love you, too. More than I ever thought possible. The whole time I was at that cabin I was more afraid of never seeing you again than I was of anything Beau was going to do. I don't want to waste time, either. I want to be your wife." I barely choke the words out before he is crushing his lips to mine and kissing me. Have I mentioned how much I love this man?

Kyle

WE FINALLY make it into the house after a very hot and heavy make out session that almost got out of hand. My body, as usual, has a mind of its own when it is up against hers. But, when I squeeze her waist and she winces in pain, I know we need to stop. While we were at the hospital, I had decided that I was going to pamper her tonight. I knew she was exhausted and probably in pain, so I thought a hot bubble bath and some cuddling would be the best medicine. I don't want Amber out of arms-reach for a long time … if ever. Now, it's all about her relaxing and trying to start putting the last two days behind her.

Once we get inside I tell Amber to head upstairs. I grab a bottle of champagne and two glasses. When I get to the bedroom, Amber is filling the tub and getting undressed. She has her back to me and I stop dead in my tracks and audibly gasp. That son of a bitch! Her entire back is covered in bruises. One of them is actually the shape of a fucking shoe. If I ever get my hands on Beau, I honestly don't think I will be able to control myself. I turn around and put the glasses on the counter. I start opening the bottle of champagne. I have to calm myself down. I don't need to upset her more than she already is. This is about helping her forget, if only for a little while. Once I get the bottle open, I pour it in the glasses, set the bottle down, and turn around to face her again. She must notice me looking at her bruises. Shit.

"I'm really okay, Kyle. I promise, it looks a lot worse than it is," she says quietly as she starts to move closer. "Let me help you out of all these clothes. They are in my way." Here I was trying to make her feel better, and she ends up making me feel better.

"I won't argue with that. But, this is supposed to be all about you."

"I say it's all about US. Let's get naked. Then grab our drinks and get in the tub and discuss our upcoming wedding. What do ya say?"

"Sounds like a perfect plan to me." She continues to help me out of my clothes as I try to keep myself under control. That is not an easy thing to do with a very beautiful, very naked Amber in front of me taking off my clothes. I grab our glasses and follow her to the tub. I get in first and she sits in front of me with her back to my chest. I hand her a glass and take one for myself.

"So what kind of wedding have you always dreamed of?" I ask, running my fingers through her silky hair. I just want to be her husband. It doesn't matter to me how it happens. The only thing I care about is that she is walking down an aisle to me. And there are "I dos" exchanged.

"Actually, ever since I was a little girl I have dreamed of a wedding here in the back yard," she says sheepishly. This surprises me. I would have pictured her wanting a church wedding. Not that either of us are religious, but her grandparents were.

"Remember when we were eight and you made me play wedding in the back yard?" I ask her. Even when I was six, I knew I was in love with her. Of course, I pretended I didn't want to play. Then, I remembered at the end you were supposed to kiss the bride. I couldn't pass that up. Yeah, even at six. I was a total horn dog. I was an early bloomer and it was all Amber's fault.

"I remember. You know the only reason I wanted to play wedding was so you would kiss me at the end." She turns and smiles at me. Damn she was a little vixen, even back then. Who would have known? Not me … seeing as it took me until ninth grade to finally realize she had feelings for me.

"Well, Princess, you can kiss me anytime you want. You don't even have to ask. These lips are yours, have always been yours." I give her a kiss on her cheek. "Do you have any idea as to when you would like this wedding?" I ask. If it were up to me, I would say tomorrow. I know she will want a little more time than that. I do want her to have the wedding she has always dreamed of. It's what she deserves. She reaches up and grabs her phone off the shelf above the tub. I rest my chin on her shoulder to see what she is doing. She pulls up a calendar app on the phone.

"Okay … today is June 25th, so how about if we set the date for Saturday, July 26 th? A month should be plenty of time to get everything together if I enlist Holly to help me." She sets the phone down and turns to look at me, waiting for my response. I am thrilled. I can deal with a month.

"I think that sounds like the perfect day to make you my wife. You just tell me what I need to do, and it's done. I want this to be everything you have ever dreamed it would be, Princess." I hold her face in my hands and brush my lips gently across hers as I say, "I love you. You are the air that I need to breathe. My heart. My everything. I can't wait to be married to you." Then, I kiss her.

Amber

IT STILL amazes me how he can be so tough and strong, but still have this sweet romantic side to him. And the way that he is kissing me right now, my God, it's the kind of kiss that makes you tingle from the top of your head to the tips of your toes. I know he is worried about my ribs and other bruises, but I need him. I need to feel him deep inside of me, have him show me just how much he loves me.

I pull back away from him slightly and look into his eyes. "Ya want to know how to really make me feel better?"

"That is something I would be interested in hearing," he says with a sexy smirk.

I bring my lips down to his ear." I want you to take me to bed and show me how much you love me." He looks like he is fighting a battle with himself about what he should do. All of a sudden, he gets out of the bathtub and wraps a towel around himself. He reaches for my hand, helps me out of the tub, and carefully dries me off. He picks me up and carries me into the bedroom and lays me down on the bed gently.

"If I hurt you please tell me, okay?" he says, so seriously. I nod and smile.

He lies down next to me and starts kissing behind my ear, then down my neck. His hand roams all along my arm, along the top of my chest, then down between my breasts. He runs it down around my belly button. He is being so gentle and sweet, and I am more than turned on. He leans over me and kisses me again. I run my hands through his hair. I want him so badly. Thank God he seems to know me better than I know myself. His cock rubs against my entrance. He kisses me so softly, and then brings his lips to my ear.

"I love you so much, Amber." He slides inside me, and nothing else matters but the two of us. He never takes his eyes off mine as he continues his slow, steady thrusts.

"I love you, too," I say as he links our fingers together and brings our arms over my head. "You feel so fucking good, Princess," he pants. He begins to thrust his hips harder and faster.

"Oh. God. Kyle!" I feel myself tighten around him, causing his release.

"Fuck. Baby!" Kyle falls to his side and pulls me with him. He kisses my forehead, eyelids, nose, and mouth.

We lie here in each other's arms for a couple hours, talking. We talk about the things that happened in the cabin. About how both of us are nervous with Beau still out there. Kyle asks me if I would not go into the center for the rest of the week. Then, he orders us some dinner from the bar and Angel drops it off. We eat in bed while we watch a movie. What a perfect, safe, relaxing night with the man I love.

CHAPTER
Eighteen

Amber

I WAKE UP to the smell of coffee and something delicious cooking downstairs. I'm surprised that I was able to sleep so soundly all night. Being held so tightly in Kyle's arms may have had something to do with that, though. I promised Kyle I would wait until Monday before going back to the center. He said Jax is handling everything just fine. He really didn't have to twist my arm to get me to agree not to go back right away. Besides, I have a wedding to plan. I slowly get out of bed and throw on some yoga pants and a tank top. I brush my teeth and use the bathroom, then saunter downstairs.

I walk into the kitchen and see Kyle cooking in only a pair of jeans, swaying his hips to the music he has playing. I sneak up behind him and cup his ass in my hands. "That is one sexy ass you have there."

"Why, thank you. I am glad you approve. Did you sleep well, Princess?" he asks with a kiss.

"I always sleep well when I am wrapped in these strong arms," I say as he holds me tighter.

"Wow, you think I have a sexy ass and strong arms. What else?" he asks with a laugh. He has the sexiest laugh. What am I saying? Every damn thing about him is sexy.

"I don't like anything about you," I say with a straight face. He looks confused. "I love everything about you, inside and out." I smile up at him. He smacks me on my ass, picks me up, and sets me down on a cool bar stool.

"I will get you some coffee. I made your favorite for breakfast … egg white omelet with bacon and cheddar," he says, proudly.

We talk about our wedding while we eat one of the best omelets I have ever had. I tell him I wanted to make Holly my Maid of Honor and Taryn and Makenna Bridesmaids. Kyle will have Paul as his Best Man with Marcus and Angel as Groomsmen. We also decide to have the reception here at the house, as well. Kyle says he will take care of getting a band and a caterer, which will help me out a lot. Before we can discuss anything further, the doorbell rings. Kyle checks who it is and I start putting the dishes in the dishwasher. When Kyle comes back into the kitchen, he is followed by Sheriff Beasley and Darcie. Before I realize what I am doing, I am running to her and hugging her tightly. I know I have taken her by surprise because I can feel her body stiffen at first. It only takes a couple seconds for her to relax and hug me back. I don't like the fact that she has slept with Kyle, and she wasn't always nice to me, but we went through something awful together.

"How are you feeling?" I ask her as I showed her and Sheriff Beasley to the kitchen table.

"I am feeling pretty good. Luckily there were no serious injuries. How about you?"

"Same here. What brings the two of you by?"

"I wanted to thank you. Sheriff Beasley said you refused to press charges. I am grateful, Amber, but you don't owe me anything. If you want to press charges, I understand. I should be punished for what I did." She looks into her coffee cup. I reach for her hand.

"Would you have done it if Beau hadn't forced you to?" I ask her.

"Of course not. It never would have crossed my mind."

"Then I don't believe you deserve any punishment for something you were forced to do. Besides, you have had enough pain and suffering over the years at the hands of Beau; you don't need any more. Are you going somewhere safe until they find him?" I hope she does. She is a much easier target than I am.

"Yeah, I am going to North Dakota to stay with my mom for a while. I am leaving tomorrow. That's another reason I came here. I wanted to say goodbye." She gives me a sad smile. It's too bad that she has to leave a place she has lived most of her life in order to feel safe. No one should have to go through that.

"I am sorry to see you go, but I am glad you are finally getting what you've been wanting. Where are you staying until you leave? Are you safe?" The second the words are out of my mouth, Kyle shoots me a look like I have completely lost my fucking mind. I wasn't really offering for her to stay here, I just want to make sure she is somewhere safe.

"She's had someone from the department with her at all times and will until she boards her plane tomorrow. She will be safe, I promise," Sheriff Beasley says to me. That makes me feel better. As far as I knew, she didn't have any family here, and who knows if she can trust any of the friends she may have had.

"I am glad you will be safe until you leave. You have my number, so keep in touch." I get up from my chair and give her another hug. I feel her shoulders shaking. Oh shit. I didn't mean to make her cry.

"You are an amazing person, Amber. Thank you for being so kind to me after everything. I am really sorry for all of it. I am sorry to you also, Kyle. I was desperate to get away from a bad situation and I thought maybe you were my ticket out." I look at Kyle hoping he is going to be nice and accept her apology. Thank goodness my man comes through with grace.

"I understand your situation now and I'm sorry that you had to go through any of that. No woman deserves to be hit. No man has a right to hit a woman, especially one he claims to love. Do us a favor and remember that when you meet someone. Don't ever let a man treat you badly again," Kyle says to her as he pats her hand.

After they leave, Kyle and I take a shower and get dressed. We decide to go down to the bar to tell Paul and Holly the good news about the wedding.

When we walk into KC's, I'm glad to see it isn't too busy. As soon as Holly notices us, she heads straight for me like a freight train. I haven't seen her since the cabin. She stayed here to keep things going for Kyle so he could concentrate on me. I really owe this girl big time. When Holly reaches me she wraps me in a hug so tight, I think she is going to break me. Kyle has to pry her off of me.

"Will you be careful, Hol? She is bruised everywhere. You need to be easy," Kyle says as he pulls her off me. Holly doesn't seem to pay him any attention.

"Why don't you go up to the bar and keep Paul company? Amber and I have some catching up to do," she says to him as she grabs my hand and pulls me to a booth in the back corner of the bar. I look back at Kyle and give him a smile. He smiles back and strolls to the bar. Holly sits me down in the booth and says she will be right back. I watch her walk to the bar. Paul pours two large Appletini's. These guys know me all too well. Paul looks at me and sees my smile. He gives me his sexy wink which earns him a smack upside the head from Kyle. I start to laugh. The two of them act just like brothers. I know Kyle's not jealous of Paul. They just like giving each other a hard time.

As soon as Holly sets the drink in front of me, I take a nice long sip and let out a contented sigh. Holly always seems to know just what I need. She has become such a great friend. I am so fortunate to have met her.

"I am only going to ask this once. So, if you want to talk about it after this you just let me know, but I am not going to push you to. I am sure everyone else already has. Okay?"

I nod my head.

"Are you really okay? I'm not talking about the bruises everyone can see on the outside. I am talking about the ones only you know about on the inside." The look that Holly gives me tells me that she has some experience with the bruises only I can see. I wonder if she will ever tell me about it. Maybe someday. I feel like I can be honest with her without her freaking out. I know Kyle's heart is in the right place and I love him even more for caring so much, but Holly doesn't treat me like I'm a porcelain doll. I am not going to break. I'm stronger than a lot of people give me credit for.

"Honestly, Holly, I have no idea. Except for the fact that he's still out there, and I can't see him just walking away and giving up, I am fine. I really don't think I've seen the last of Beau Hartly," I tell her.

She nods her head. "I've known men like him, and I think you're right. You have a shit load of people who love you and will do anything to protect you. You do realize that, right?" I just nod in confirmation, my eyes burning with unshed tears. I still can't believe that I've made so many wonderful friends in such a short time of being back here. "We're all watching out for you, Amber. I promise you, that man is going to pay for what he did to you, especially if Kyle and Paul get their hands on him."

She comes over to my side of the booth, puts her arm around me, and gives me a gentle squeeze. I take another long sip of my drink. Now, for the reason we came here, a much happier topic. I tell her all about the wedding, the date of July 26th, and that I'm enlisting her to help plan it. She squeals and claps her hands like a little kid. It is so funny, I don't think I've ever seen her so excited. I look over at the guys and they just smile and shake their heads.

"I also had something else I needed to ask you …" I wait until she calms down and faces me. "Will you be my Maid of Honor?" I ask. Oh. My. God! The squeal that left this woman just about blew out my eardrums.

"Of course I will," she says, tears streaming down her face. "I've never really had a best friend before you. I couldn't have chosen a better one if I tried."

Now she has me crying. We must look like a couple of lunatics over here. Paul and Kyle are at the bar laughing their asses off at the two of us. So, I did what any mature adult would do. I stuck my tongue out at them.

Kyle

IT'S BEEN over a week since the cabin and Amber went back to work at the center. I convinced her to let me hire a security guard. At first, she wasn't going to allow it, so I had to think of some way to change her mind. I used the one thing she couldn't possibly say no to … the kids. I told her that if Beau came around, she wasn't the only one in danger. By the look on her face, I know she knew it was true. I had to promise to use private security dressed in plain clothes with no visible weapons. I had absolutely no problem with any of that.

Someone is guarding every entrance to the center and a surveillance van just around the corner is tapped into the security cameras in the center. Now, I feel much better about her going back to work. Although there have been no signs of Beau, I know that bastard is still out there, just waiting for the right time to make a move. There is no way he just disappeared. So, until we catch him, Amber is not going to be alone.

As for today, Holly set up a joint bachelor/bachelorette party at the bar. Amber wasn't too keen on the idea at first, seeing as our last Sunday party ended with my truck being blown up. But, Holly didn't give her a choice. She listed solid reasons as to why it was a great idea and I hired the same security detail to make her feel safer. I was not letting Beau take this away from her. Not for a second.

As always, Marty and Clark insisted on cooking the food. We are keeping everything clean, so everyone's kids are here, too. We have the karaoke machine set up for the kids and whoever else wants to sing. Everyone seems to be having a really good time which we all really needed. Amber and I weren't the only ones that had been affected by Beau. Every one of these people here today loves her, and they were worried sick about her. They are all still worried about her. At least for one day we can forget about what could be lurking out just around the corner.

I love seeing Amber happy and having fun, especially after all of the stress lately. All afternoon she has been laughing and smiling. Holly, Taryn, Anna, Makenna, and even Leena are all pulling a giggling Amber up on stage. Oh, this should be good. These women are already about three sheets to the wind. Everyone in the bar has his or her eyes on the stage, and they are thinking the exact same thing I am. Holly goes over and punches a song into the karaoke machine. All the girls line up with Amber in the middle. As *Girls Just Want to Have Fun* starts to play, they all start laughing and dancing. The only one I can see is Amber. She is always beautiful, but when she is carefree, laughing, and dancing, she is absolutely gorgeous. I can't believe in less than three weeks she is going to be my wife. How did I get lucky enough to have a second chance with her? She looks right at me and winks as she raises her hands above her head and moves her perfect little hips. If she keeps this up, I am going drag her ass into my office and watch those perfect little hips wiggle while I take her against the door. My dick throbs just thinking about it.

"Why do I get the feeling we are going to be carrying our women home, passed out, before it's even dark outside?" Paul says with a laugh as he sits next to me at the bar.

"I think you're right. I give them maybe another hour. Hour and a half, tops," I say as I watch all the girls stumble around the stage trying to pick another song. "I'm glad we didn't spend money on entertainment. This is way better," I say, tipping my beer in the direction of the women now singing *It's Raining Men* and pointing to all of us. My stomach is starting to hurt from laughing so hard.

My good mood is cut short when Marcus comes over to the table and tells us to follow him to the office. He looks pretty upset. He also grabs Angel and Beasley on the way back. Shit … this can't be good. As soon as we are all piled in my office, Marcus closes the door and places a brown envelope on the desk. Amber's name is written on it.

"I went outside to get some toys out of the car for Chase, and when I was coming back in I noticed this envelope sitting against the door. I didn't open it, but I'm pretty sure I know who it's from," he says through clenched teeth. Marcus is a quiet, even-tempered guy, but the day he found out Amber was missing, he went a little crazy. Then, the first day he saw her with a swollen face full of cuts and bruises, he stormed into the kitchen of the bar and started throwing things. It took Paul and Angel both to calm him down. He grew up with a very abusive father, so it was difficult for him to see Amber like that and not be able to anything about it. I grab the envelope and carefully open it. I pull out the handwritten letter .The more of it I read, the more it pisses me off.

> *Dear Amber,*
> *I wanted to make sure you knew that I haven't forgotten about you. I've been keeping a very close eye on you. I promised we would be together and I intend to keep that promise. When the time is right, I will be coming for you. I know Kyle has been trying to keep you away from me, but I will find my opportunity to get to you alone. So, don't worry, you won't have to be without me for much longer. See you soon, my love.*
> *Love, Beau*

"*Mother fucker!*" I scream as my fist slams through the wall behind my desk. My blood boils. I know this isn't accomplishing anything, but I can't control myself. "*Son of a bitch!*" I slam my fist into the wall again. Before I can put a third hole in my wall, Paul grabs me and pulls me over to the couch and sits me down.

"Calm the fuck down!" he yells, still holding my arms. "Letting your temper get the best of you is not going to help Amber," he says a little calmer than he starts out. They all read the letter. At least I am not the only one who is pissed. It looks like Angel's head is going to pop off his shoulders. Beasley keeps putting his hand on his gun at his side like he wants to shoot someone. Paul seems to be the calmest, but I know better. He is just really good at hiding it. I can see it in his eyes. If Beau was in front of him right now, he would be a dead man in seconds.

"I can't let him get to her. I promised I would always protect her, and he already hurt her once. I can't let him do it again." I know I sound like a sniveling little pussy, but I don't care. The only thing that matters is Amber.

Beasley finally speaks up. "First, we are not going to tell her about this letter. Do you all understand me?" He looks around the room, waiting for everyone to confirm he was heard. Everyone nods their head in agreement. "Second, she will not, under any circumstances, be left alone. Not even for a second." Beasley looks straight at me. "From this point moving forward, get your security guys to tail her everywhere she goes. Always have eyes on her. Even at home, have them stand watch at night while you are sleeping. That is also something she doesn't need to know. She has a wedding coming up and I want her happy as well as safe. I don't care if one of us has to go with the girls to pick out dresses. One of us will be with her all the time." We all agree with him.

I ask Marcus to explain everything to Clark and Marty, but make sure none of the girls are listening. I ask Angel if he can get Jax in here for me, I need him to know what's going on so he can keep an eye on her at the center. I am not all that thrilled with keeping this from Amber, but I can do it until the wedding so she can be happy. Jax is a different story. It is going to be very hard to make him understand that keeping this from her is the best thing. If Beau still isn't caught by the time the wedding rolls around, I'll tell her everything. At the very most, three weeks.

When Jax comes in I show him the letter and explain what Beasley wanted. Just like I thought, he isn't thrilled.

"She has a right to know this psycho is still after her. You can't keep this from her," Jax argues. Beasley isn't having it. I have never seen Beasley like this before.

"Now, you listen here. No one is telling that girl anything until after her wedding. I am going to do everything I can to make sure she has the perfect day she has always dreamed of. I couldn't save her parents so they could be here for her, but I will make damn sure she has a perfect wedding." What the hell was he talking about when he said he couldn't save her parents? He must notice the confusion clearly painted on my face.

"After the wedding, I will explain it all to Amber. I think it is about time she knows the truth about what really happened to her parents," he says somberly. This doesn't sound good. We tell Jax about all the extra hidden security and all of us making sure she isn't left alone. He finally agrees to help us look after her while keeping his mouth shut.

"I really hope you two know what you're doing," Jax says as he stands up and walks out of the room. I look over at Beasley. God, I hope we do, too.

CHAPTER
Nineteen

Amber

I ROLL OVER in bed, afraid to open my eyes. My head hurts so badly. How many Appletini's did I drink last night? I squint my eyes open a little. Big mistake. Before I can throw my pillow over my head, I hear Kyle chuckle from the doorway. I open one eye and look over at his handsome, smiling face. Why doesn't he look as bad as I feel? It was his bachelor party, too. I notice I have on one of Kyle's t-shirts and my panties. How the hell did he manage to undress me without me knowing it? Oh well, at least he brought me coffee. I guess I can forgive him for looking so damn good.

"Good morning, Princess. How are you feeling this morning, my little lush?" he says with a laugh as he dodges me trying to smack his arm.

"The last thing I remember is singing with the girls. After that, it's a blank," I say with a groan.

"You don't remember anything after that? Are you sure?" he asks a little too seriously. Oh no, what did I do?

"What did I do? Please tell me I didn't make a total fool of myself in front of all of our friends," I plead with him. He looks at me sympathetically. I am never going to be able to show my face around our friends ever again.

"It wasn't that bad, really. Before we left the bar you got on stage, picked up the mic, and said, 'Kyle, I'm ready for you to take me home and fuck me senseless.' You got quite a few laughs. All the guys were trying to pretend they were me. I had to fight them off to get you out the door," he says, laughing. I throw my arm over my face. Great. He takes my coffee out of my hands and places it on the nightstand next to the bed. He leans over me and kisses and nips my ear.

"Too bad you have to get in the shower to get ready to go dress shopping with the girls," he whispers in my ear. "If we had time, I would fill your request. I'd fuck you against the door, on the floor, in the shower, against a wall, on the stairs. Senseless. You wouldn't know how to handle it." Oh my. The way he says that as he kisses my ear and neck sends instant heat and wetness between my legs. I reach over and grab my phone. I type a quick text to Holly.

> **Me:** *Give me an extra 45 minutes before you pick me up please ;)*
> **Holly:** *LOL! Is Kyle giving it to u good? Ha Ha ;)*

Gotta love Holly. I place my phone down and turn to him, kissing him lightly as I grab his very hard cock through his boxers. I love how much just kissing me turns him on.

"I just bought us an extra forty-five minutes. How about you join me in the shower. You can fuck me against the wall," I say with a grin as I slide my hand inside his boxers. As soon as I touch his bare skin, he moans. I have no idea how he manages it, but he is able to get off the bed with me in his arms and carry me into the bathroom. I squeal and wrap both arms around his neck, afraid I'll fall. Without breaking our kiss, he turns the shower on, and then gently sets me on the floor. He grabs the bottom of the t-shirt and quickly pulls it up over my head. The way he looks at me, all dark and smoldering, makes me instantly wet. His lips then come down on my shoulder, and he slowly kisses along my collarbone. He keeps kissing down along the top of my breast. I run my hands through his silky hair. He sucks and licks the nipple of, first, my right breast before moving to the left to pay it the same attention. His hands reach down between my legs and I moan in anticipation. Instead of touching me, though, he rips my panties off of me. Before I have a chance to reach for them, he has his boxers off. He bends down, grabs my ass with both hands, and lifts me up. I quickly wrap my legs around his waist as he kisses me again and walks us into the steamy shower. I close the door behind us. He reaches down between my legs and runs his fingers along my entrance.

"Do you know how fucking hot it is that you are always so wet and ready for me, Princess?" he growls as he gently bites on my neck.

"Well, if it's anything like how hot it is that you are always hard and ready for me, then yes, I do know," I say as I position myself just right and slide down over him.

"Mmm ... Princess," he groans as he turns us around and slams my back against the wall. Finally, the old Kyle is back. The one that doesn't treat me like glass. I really missed him. He thrusts inside me so hard, I know I'm going to have a hard time walking later. Not that I am complaining. It feels way too good to care about being a little bow-legged later.

"Is this what you had in mind, baby?" he asks as he grips my hips tighter.

"Yes ... but ... even ... better." It is getting hard to think. I can feel myself getting so close. And by the sounds coming from Kyle, he is, too. He slows his pace enough to bring his lips to my ear. He knows that whispering or breathing in my ear is enough to make me explode.

"Come with me, Princess." His deep voice tinged with need is all it takes to send me flying over the edge. My head falls forward and I am screaming his name as I feel myself tighten around him. He is right there with me.

"Oh. Fuck. Baby. I love you," he says as he stills and drops to the floor with me still on his lap. I snuggle into him as close as I can.

"I love you, too." I rest my head on his shoulder and sigh in contentment. Life does not get better than this. After a few moments, Kyle stands us up. He slowly and carefully washes every single inch of me, including my hair. When he is done, I try to return the favor, but he kisses me sweetly and hands me a towel.

"Get ready so you can go find that beautiful dress you are going to marry me in," he says as he gives me his panty-dropping smile. If he wants me to get dressed, he really needs to stop looking at me like that. Reluctantly, I get dressed. Half an hour later, I'm kissing Kyle goodbye at the front door.

I climb into the front seat of Holly's SUV, and I am shocked to see Paul driving. Holly and Taryn are in the back seat. He notices my surprised look and laughs at me.

"Kyle put me in charge of the tuxes. Holly said the colors of the ties and shit have to match the Bridesmaid dresses. So, I thought I could pick all that out with you guys, seeing as I don't know the first damn thing about it. Do you know how many different styles of tuxes there are? I don't want to screw up your big day by picking ugly tuxes." He gives me a sheepish grin. "You wouldn't want us up there looking like the guys from *Dumb & Dumber* would you?" He laughs. With the killer smiles these boys have, I'm not surprised they always get their way.

"Well, I guess for today you're just one of the girls," I say with a smile.

"Oh goody! This is going to be so much fun!" Paul says in the girliest voice he can manage. He keeps us in stitches all the way to Miami. The drive is about an hour and a half long, but Miami is the biggest city around. If I can't find a dress there, then I am not going to find one anywhere.

The first boutique we stop at makes me smile when I see the name. To no one in particular, I say, "Did Kyle pick out this place?"

Taryn, who doesn't talk much, speaks up. "No, actually I found it online. Isn't the name perfect? When I looked at some of their designs they seemed to specialize in what you have in mind." I give her a smile that says how much I appreciate how thoughtful she is. The name of the boutique is "Princess Weddings." Fitting, right? Ever since I was a little girl I have always wanted to wear a wedding dress that made me look like a princess from a fairy tale. I was obsessed with Disney princesses as a child, hence Kyle's nickname for me.

We all pile out of the SUV and head inside. The place is huge and breathtaking. There are crystal chandeliers hanging everywhere. The flooring is white and grey marble. The walls are painted a pastel pink with beautiful photos of women in even more beautiful wedding gowns. There is a sitting area off to the right with cream colored leather couches and marble coffee tables. A very tall, handsome man steps out from behind a white satin curtain. He looks like a Greek God. He has black hair with eyes so blue, they look like they are glowing. His skin is a golden olive color … and the muscles. My Lord, the muscles. Unfortunately, he only seems to have eyes for Paul. Which all of us find quite amusing.

"My name is Zeus." He is even named after a Greek God. "Which one of you lovely ladies is our bride?" he asks, still eyeballing Paul. My stomach is going to hurt so badly by the time I get home from laughing so hard. Everyone points to me. Zeus takes my hand and leads me to a couch. There are a bunch of books on the coffee table in front of me.

"You start looking through these. When you see something you like, write down the number. Once you choose a couple to start trying on, I will have a good idea of what you are looking for and we can go from there. I will go and get you all some champagne while you start looking." He winks at Paul as he passes, and we all burst out laughing ... even Paul.

After I choose five dresses from the book, I start trying them on. By the time I am trying on the third one, Zeus has a rack full of dresses for me. Two bottles of champagne and twenty dresses later, I'm getting frustrated. All of the dresses I have tried on are beautiful, they just aren't "The One." I feel bad that Paul and the girls are probably bored out of their minds. Paul has chosen the tuxes and the girls have picked the bridesmaid gowns. My only stipulation was the color. I had to have purple. It is my favorite color, after all. The girls chose a simple, deep plum strapless satin dress. It's floor-length, and it is gorgeous. The dress is very elegant and would be cool in the summer heat. The best part is that it could be worn again to other occasions. They are perfect. The tuxes are traditional black with white shirts and bow ties. The vests are the same color plum as the girls' dresses.

Zeus yells into the dressing room. "I think I've found what you are looking for, doll. Try this one." I take the dress he slides through the opening of the door and hang it up. Before I can get it off the hanger, I already know this is it. I quickly put the dress on. I stand in front of the mirror with tears in my eyes. This is the perfect dress. The one I have imagined since I was little. It is white satin with a V-neck that is off the shoulders. The train is long but will come apart for the reception. The skirt is very full. The skirt and bodice are adorned with hand-sewn beading. The back buttons from my waist to the middle of my back. It is just beautiful. I call Zeus in to help me button it.

"You are stunning. This is the one, isn't it, doll? I knew we would find it!" he squeals in excitement. I walk out of the dressing room, anxious to show everyone. As I step out and stand in front of them, they all stop talking and their mouths hang open. I immediately start looking down, wondering what is wrong. I thought it was perfect. Did it look better in the mirror to me than it really does?

"You don't like it?" I ask nervously. I notice Holly and Taryn start crying and shaking their heads. Were they saying they didn't like it? I am starting to freak out a little. When Paul steps up to me and grabs my hands and twirls me around so everyone can see the dress from all sides, I get the feeling that I am wrong.

"You are the most beautiful bride I have ever seen. My friend is one lucky man. He is going to be blown away when he sees you coming down that aisle," he says as he places a kiss on my cheek. I start crying as Holly and Taryn come over to hug me, still shaking their heads.

Finally, Holly finds her voice. "Oh my God, Amber, you are beautiful. That dress is perfect. I didn't mean to scare you. I was speechless." She cries as she hugs me again.

"Yeah … what she said." Poor Taryn still can't speak. Have I mentioned that I have the best friends ever?

We all pick out shoes and jewelry. The girls choose black pumps and black pearl necklaces and earrings. I go with white pumps and diamond earrings that dangle from my ears and a v-shaped diamond necklace. We find a diamond tiara with a veil that lies beautifully at the back of my head. I plan on wearing my hair up, so it should work perfectly.

We pay for our things and head out. We are all starving and decide to have lunch before we head back to Oakville. It has been a really amazing day. I was worried at first with Paul coming along that it would be strange having a guy with us, but he ended up making it so much better.

Kyle

BEASLEY AND I have been trying everything we can think of to track down Beau. How this fucker can stay hidden in such a small town is beyond me. I think old Beasley is more determined than I am to get the son of a bitch. I am really curious to know what it is that has him feeling responsible for the death of Amber's parents. I've tried a couple times to get him to tell me, but he keeps saying after the wedding he will tell Amber and I together. He must think she will take it hard if he is afraid it will ruin the wedding for her.

At least I know she is safe and having a good time today in Miami. At the party last night Paul and I came up with the idea of him going with the girls today to watch over them. Even though the security guys would be following close behind, I felt better knowing Paul was right there within arm's reach at all times. There was no way Beau could get anywhere near her with Paul there. Paul was also worried about Holly's safety, seeing that she is always with Amber, especially now with all of the wedding planning they are doing. We thought it would be best that she knew what was going on so she could be alert to her surroundings. I don't know the whole story, but Holly had a very abusive ex-husband, so she has dealt with this shit before. Plus, she doesn't go anywhere without her gun on her. From what I have seen from a couple visits to the shooting range, she is an expert marksman. I sure as hell wouldn't want to be on the barrel end of her gun.

Paul has been texting me all day to let me know how Amber is doing. It sounds like they are all having a great time. I am so grateful for my friend. He has taken her in like she is his little sister. There is no doubt in my mind that he would protect her just as fiercely as he would Holly. Shit, from what I have witnessed these last few weeks, all my bandmates would do the same for her. It just proves the four of us have a bond more like brothers. I would do anything to protect them or anyone they loved, as well.

It's like Angel said to me the other day … who couldn't love Amber? You can't know her and not instantly love her and feel like you want to keep her safe and happy. I must have looked at him funny when he said it, because he quickly threw in, "Ya know, like a sister." I know what he meant, though. I fell for her instantly. You just can't help it.

I got a lot accomplished today. I hired a caterer for the reception. Amber said she didn't want anything pretentious and fancy, but she did want food people didn't get to eat every day. So, I found a caterer that brings in these huge grills and cooks the food right there like a giant barbecue. Nothing pretentious about that. The menu, however, will consist of bacon-wrapped filets, scallops, shrimp, lobster tails, and, for the kids, hot dogs and burgers. There will also be all kinds of sides and salads. I think I was able to get exactly what she had in mind.

I also hired a band. When we were in L.A. we played a lot of clubs with a group of guys called Deuce. They had a sound similar to us, and we all got along great. I called Jake, their singer, and they just happen to be on a break right now and were more than happy to come and do this for us. It will be awesome to see them all again.

Though the best accomplishment of today, which will be a total surprise to Amber, is booking our honeymoon. We were watching some travel channel on television the other night, and they were doing a show on Bora Bora. Amber fell in love with the place. I just booked us two weeks in one of those villas that sit above the ocean. It has 1022 square feet and a private water-side balcony. There is also a glass floor with viewing panels and a private swimming pool. She is going to love it. I printed out pictures and put them in a box. Then, I wrapped the box in sparkly purple wrapping paper with a big bow. I am going to give it to her during our reception. She thinks we are going to wait and plan a honeymoon for some time next year, but I think getting the hell away from here is the best thing for both of us, even if it is only for two weeks. I already spoke with Jax and he said he could handle the center while she was gone. I have to admit, he has really stepped up lately. I think he is finally realizing he doesn't have a chance with Amber. Hopefully someone else will come along for him. He isn't that bad of a guy when he's not trying to steal my girl.

CHAPTER
Twenty

Amber

$\mathcal{I}$T WAS about six o'clock in the evening when we pull up to my house and I notice Kyle's truck isn't here yet. As much as I don't want to admit it, I am a little nervous about being alone. I am trying to think of a way to ask Paul and Holly to come in without it sounding like I'm scared. I don't want to add any more stress on Kyle. I knew that the fact that Beau was still out there was enough for him to deal with, he didn't need to know I was a nervous wreck all the time, too. Luckily, Holly knows me all too well.

"How about Paul and I come in for a while? We can call Kyle and have him bring home some dinner from the bar. It would give the four of us a chance to go over our wedding checklists and see what is left to be done." She isn't asking, she is telling.

"That sounds good to me as long as you guys aren't too tired."

"Nope, not at all," Paul says as he turns off his truck.

As I get closer to the front porch, I can see a huge bouquet of flowers in a crystal vase. Paul takes my keys from me to unlock the door while I grab the flowers. I assume they are from Kyle, but I still can't wait to open the card. I place the vase on the counter in the kitchen and pull the card out. Paul is on the phone with Kyle telling him we were at the house and to bring home some food. As I pull the card from the envelope, I realize the flowers aren't from Kyle. Beau. Everything around me starts to fade in and out. I hear the vase crash to the floor as I follow it. The last words I hear are Paul's as he yells to Kyle. "Fuck the food! Get home now!" Then everything is black.

"Princess ... wake up. Please, baby? Open your eyes." I can hear Kyle and he sounds a little panicked. Then I feel something wet and cold on my forehead. As I open my eyes I can see the relief flash over Kyle's face. I smile at him to try and reassure him that I am okay. I think I am okay anyway.

"What the hell happened?" I ask.

"You fainted, Princess," Kyle says as I try to get up from the kitchen floor. Kyle has other ideas, though. He picks me up and carries me into the living room and sits me on the couch. Paul and Holly are close behind. Holly with a wet cloth in her hand' and Paul with a glass of water in his. I take a sip of the water and look at the three guilty faces staring back at me.

"Okay ... what's going on? You three look awful guilty. Who is going to start explaining?" I say sternly and look between the three of them.

"I will," says Sheriff Beasley from out of nowhere. Where did he come from? Why is he here? Oh no, the flowers ... they were from him.

"Let me see that card again," I say to Holly who is trying to hide it behind her back. Obviously, she is doing a terrible job of it. Beasley nods to her and she hands it to me. I take a deep breath and then read it.

> *My Amber,*
>
> *I told you I was watching your every move just waiting for the right moment. You were beautiful today in that dress. Such a shame you want to waste such beauty on someone so unworthy as Kyle. We will be together soon and you can wear it for me instead. I am the only one who can understand the pain you suffered when you lost your mother. We share a bond that will hold us together through eternity. I will come for you very soon and take you away from all of those people who pretend to love you. Together we will be reunited*

with the loved ones we have lost. He can't keep you from
me forever.
Love,
Beau

I drop the card and quickly run to the bathroom. I barely make it before I'm emptying my stomach into the toilet bowl. Once I am sure there is nothing left, I flush the toilet and stand. I go to the sink, rinse my mouth out, and splash some water on my face. Time to go find out what everyone has been hiding from me and why. Do they think I can't handle whatever has been going on? Well, I'll show them. I march my ass into the living room. They are all looking at me like they are puppies that just peed on the carpet, and I am getting ready to scold them and rub their noses in it. Kyle starts to get up and walk to me, but I throw my hand up and stop him dead in his tracks.

"Obviously the four of you have been keeping something from me. First, I want to know why." I put my hand up to keep anyone from answering. "Do you all think I am some weak little girl who can't handle whatever is going on? And second, I want to know *everything* you have been keeping from me. Now, you may speak." I take a seat across the room in the recliner and wait. Beasley stands up and starts pacing. He looks nervous. I have known him my whole life and I have never ever seen him nervous.

"I was the one who insisted that we keep the first letter from Beau a secret. It had nothing to do with thinking you couldn't handle it. I know you can. You have been dealt a shit hand; you have lost more in your twenty-five years than most have in a lifetime. Yet, you are still a strong, sweet, caring, and loving woman. I have seen people turn cold and bitter over a hell of a lot less." He is getting a little choked up. I have never seen him emotional. What the fuck is going on? He pulls the stool in front of my chair and sits on it and continues. "I didn't want anything to darken your mood and ruin your chance for the perfect wedding day you have always wanted and deserved. I promised your grandparents that if anything happened to them I would make sure you were taken care of, and I plan to keep that promise." He looks at me, letting everything sink in. I can understand that they all want me to be happy. That is one of the reasons why I love everyone in this room. They all care about me as much as I do them. I can't fault them for that.

"I want to see the other letter." I look at Beasley because I assume he is the ringleader. Everyone else seems to do what he says. He nods and pulls a folded piece of paper from his pocket. He hands it to me. I take a deep breath. I have to be strong. No puking after reading this one. I slowly open it up and begin reading it.

Once I'm finished, I fold it back up and hand it back to Beasley.

"What did he mean when he said he is the only one who can understand the pain I suffered when I lost my mother? I lost both parents, not just my mother. And what is this bond he is talking about?" I ask Beasley. He seems to have all of the answers. He looks at Kyle and nods toward me. Kyle stands and walks to the back of my chair. Why do I get the feeling I am really not going to like where this story is heading? Kyle places his hands on my shoulders and gives them a gentle reassuring squeeze.

"When Beau was about three his father, Kent, found out that his mother, Alice, cheated on him. During the affair that Alice had, she became pregnant with Beau, but for three years Kent thought Beau was his son. When he found out he wasn't … he went crazy. He ended up shooting Alice and then himself." He never takes his eyes off of me. That was a terrible thing to happen, but I still don't understand what this has to do with me.

"How does that have anything to do with my parents dying in a car accident?" I ask. He looks down at his lap and then back to me again.

"Your parents didn't really die in a car accident, Amber. Your grandparents told you that because they didn't want you to grow up with the truth stigmatizing you everywhere you went. We were trying to protect you."

"We? How are you involved in all of this? And what the fuck really happened to my parents?" I scream. I know I am losing my cool. I am scared and confused. I feel betrayed by the people I love the most in this world. I think I have the right to be upset. I have been lied to my whole life. The only person telling me the truth is a fucking psychopath whvo wants to kill me. I look at Kyle.

"Wait … did you know about all of this?" I ask. I am not sure if I want to know. If he did know, I don't know if I could ever forgive him for keeping it from me. He moves in between Beasley and I and grabs my face.

"I swear to you, I knew nothing about any of this until now. The only thing I kept from you was the first letter," he says, desperate for me to believe him. And, I do. I can see it in his eyes. I nod. He sits on the arm of the chair and puts an arm around me. We both look to Beasley to continue. He takes a deep breath.

"Meredith, your mom, was a wonderful woman. And Charles was a good man, too. Charles was gone a lot on the fishing boats, and your mom started getting lonely. She met someone, fell in love with him, and had an affair. Thing is … she still loved Charles also. The other man walked away so that your mom didn't have to make the choice herself. Charles never found out. When you were two, you fell and split your head open. You needed a blood transfusion. When Charles went to give blood, they found out his didn't match." He stops and looks at me. Oh my God. My dad wasn't my dad. That means my grandparents weren't my grandparents … by blood anyway. Who the hell was my father then? I look up at Beasley, and just like that, it hit me.

"You're my father, aren't you?" I ask in almost a whisper. I am not sure how I feel about it all. On one hand, I still have some family who are alive. I have always loved Beasley, and so did my grandparents, even though they knew the truth. On the other hand, my mother is a cheater. And Charles, my so-called father, what did he end up doing?

"Yes, Amber. I am your father. I have known since you were two, along with your grandparents. But, what I am about to tell you next is the reason we never said anything. We didn't want to bring you any more pain or make you think somehow you were to blame for what happened to your mom and Charles. After the hospital told your mom and Charles about the blood test not matching, she told him everything. He left to come find me, but your mom tried to stop him. She jumped in his truck with him, and he got so angry that she was trying to stop him, he reached in the glove box, pulled out his gun, and shot her and then himself. Your mom lived for a couple hours, but her injuries were too severe. There was nothing they could do. Your grandparents didn't want you to be traumatized by all of this, so they asked me to keep the fact that I was your father to myself until I felt you were old enough to handle it. I was just glad they allowed me to be a part of your life as you grew up. They were wonderful people. Your grandfather was my best friend." He stands up and walks to the kitchen. I assume it is because he didn't want any of us to see him cry. I am numb. I don't know what to say to anyone. I have no idea how I feel. I want to cry. I want to break something. I need to process all of this.

"Why don't you go up and take a nice hot bath. I will see everyone out and be up in a little while."

I disappear before I have to see Beasley again.

Kyle

I WATCHED Amber haul ass up the stairs. My poor girl. I have to say, she handled this a hell of a lot better than I would have. If I didn't know Beasley so well I would've thought he was full of shit. That story is like something you would watch on some made for TV movie. Not something that happens in real life. I need to figure out the best way to get her through this and to make our wedding perfect for her.

Paul and Holly come out of the living room, heading to the front door.

"Hey, is she okay?" Paul asks as Holly looks over at Beasley like she wants to give him a big hug.

"I think she will be. That's a lot of shit to process all at once. Can you check with the security guys when you leave and make sure they have people all around the house tonight? He keeps getting too damn close."

"You got it. Call if there's anything else you need. Anytime, day or night," he says and pulls me in for a hug. I don't know what I would do without him. He has been there for me through a lot of shit.

"Paul and I will take care of the bar in the morning. Stay with Amber if she needs you. We can handle the bar as long as we need to." Holly kisses my cheek. "Tell her to call me if she needs me for anything."

"You guys are awesome. Thank you for everything. What would we do without the two of you?" I say to them both. In true Holly fashion, she has a comeback.

"Oh, you couldn't do anything without the two of us. And yes, we are awesome, that's why you love us." She smiles at me knowing it will make me smile. Then, they head out the door. Now I have to go and talk to Beasley. This is not going to be easy. I feel torn. It must have been hard all these years for Beasley to know Amber was his daughter and not tell her. At the same time, though, Amber has been an adult for a while now, and she should have been told. When I walk into the kitchen, Beasley quickly turns around. As soon as he sees it is only me, a sad expression comes across his face. He must have been hoping it would be Amber.

"She needs a little time to let all of this sink in. That was a huge amount of stuff to hear all at once," I tell him as I reach for the bottle of whiskey and two shot glasses. I sit next to him on a stool and pour each of us a shot. "To our girl," I say as I lift my glass to his. We both down the shots, and I pour two more.

"I really didn't want anything to ruin her wedding day. That is the only reason I wanted to wait to tell her. I never wanted to keep it a secret after Charles and Meredith died. Gene and Ima were such good people, and I thought they knew better than I did. I just hope someday Amber can forgive me," he says sadly as he drinks the second shot.

"You know the type of person she is just as well as I do. Once the shock wears off and she realizes you were all acting out of love, she will understand. Her ability to forgive and her big heart are only some of the reasons I love her so much," I say with that goofy fucking grin I always get when I talk about Amber. Beasley noticed too, because he looks at me and chuckles.

"I stayed here after she left because I knew she would be back here."

"How could you know that?" I ask him. Hell, I didn't even know it. I had always hoped she would come back, but I hadn't been holding my breath.

"Because, just like her grandparents saw it, so did I. The two of you were destined to be together. I knew when you bought the bar that someday she'd be back." He smiles, stands up, and pats me on the shoulder. "Take care of her. Call me and let me know how she's doing will ya?" I nod as I follow him to the door. He turns and looks toward the stairs, hoping to see her before walking out the door, looking like he lost his best friend. I close the door behind him and lock it up.

I drink the shot of whiskey I left on the counter. I put the glasses in the sink and put the bottle away. I pour two glasses of wine and go upstairs. I walk into the bathroom and Amber is in the tub crying. It breaks my heart to see her so upset and to know there is nothing I can do about it. I set the glasses down on the edge of the tub and quickly get undressed to join her. I slip into the warm water behind Amber and wrap her in my arms. I don't say a word. I just hold her tight and let her get it all out. I don't know what else to do. There is nothing I can say that will make any of this better for her. After a while, she starts to calm down.

"Princess, the water is pretty cold. How about we get out and have a glass of wine in bed?" I ask, still holding her tight. She just nods against my chest. I ease myself out from under her and dry off. I help her out and dry her from head to toe. I pick her up and carry her to bed. I hand Amber a glass of wine then crawl into bed next to her. We sit in silence for a long time. I don't want to push her to talk if she isn't ready. I assume she will talk to me about everything when she is ready, and I'm right.

"There are so many different things I am feeling at once, and it is confusing the hell out of me." I know her well enough to know she doesn't want a response. She wants to get it all out. "I am angry that my grandparents kept this from me my whole life. That for twenty-three years my father has been right in front of me, and I didn't know it. Then, when they died I was left to think I had no family left. That I was all alone. Beasley was at the funeral. Why didn't he tell me then? There was nobody left to stop him." She looks over at me. Now she wants some answers. Shit. These aren't questions I have answers to.

"Babe, as far as your grandparents go … they loved you more than anything else in this world. They thought keeping this from you would protect you somehow. You know in your heart that they would never do anything to intentionally hurt you." She nods her head. "As for Beasley, those are questions you need to ask him. I know it's not going to be easy, but I think it will be good for you. You have always loved him, and finding out that you do still have family is a good thing. At least you already know what kind of guy he is," I say to her, hoping I am not being too pushy. Beasley is a really good guy, and the both of them deserve to be happy.

"You're right. I'll call him in the morning and see if he will meet me at the bar for lunch."

"Why the bar? Wouldn't you rather be someplace more private?"

"I think I will be more comfortable there with you, Holly, and Paul around for support." She smiles up at me. I'm glad she knows she has people who care about her that she can lean on when she needs it.

"Sounds good. It's been a long day, let's get some sleep," I say as I grab her glass and set it on the night stand next to mine. I flip off the lamp and pull her to me. She rests her head on my chest and I hold her tightly.

"I feel so safe and loved right here in your arms," she says as she places a kiss on my chest.

"I do love you. I love you more than you will ever know, and I would die to keep you safe, Princess." I kiss the top of her head as I feel her tears fall on my chest.

"I am so lucky to have you in my life."

"No, Princess, I am the lucky one. Now, let's get some sleep. Sweet dreams." She snuggles up as close as she can to me. Not that I am complaining. The closer I am to her, the better. It doesn't take long for her to fall asleep. I am glad she is getting some rest. Tonight was pretty stressful for her. Maybe after she talks to Beasley and gets some of the answers she is looking for, it will be easier for her. Honestly, Beasley being her father isn't what is keeping me awake. It's that son of a bitch Beau. That card attached to the flowers freaked me out just as badly as it did her. He intends to kill her if he gets to her. Beau has been able to stay hidden while still watching her. It's like I'm up against a fucking ghost.

CHAPTER
Twenty-One

Amber

I WAKE UP before Kyle, and I just lie here, listening to him breathe. I didn't think it was possible to love someone as much as I love him. I know all of this mess has to be causing him a great deal of stress, as well. You could never tell by looking at him, though. Always strong and supportive. It's hard to believe in a couple weeks I will be marrying my Prince Charming. Just thinking about it makes me smile. That is what I am going to focus on. I can't change the past. I loved my grandparents, and they loved me. They thought keeping what happened to my parents a secret was protecting me. There was nothing malicious about it. They weren't trying to hurt me. And, Kyle was right about Beasley. He is a good guy. He wouldn't hurt me either. It's seems funny now, I always thought of him like an uncle. He went to every school play, recital, science fair, you name it. If it was something my grandparents were at, so was he. Now, I understand why. On the way home from Miami yesterday I was telling Holly and Paul that I was going to ask Beasley if he would walk me down the aisle. Now that couldn't be more perfect.

I look over at the clock and see that it's almost ten. I grab my phone and send a text to Beasley.

Me: *Can you meet me at KC's at 11:30?*
Beasley: *Of course. See you then.*

I ease out of bed and get into the shower. As I am washing my hair, I try to decide whether or not I am nervous about my meeting with Beasley. I am a little but they aren't bad nerves. How do I act around him now? Does he expect me to call him dad? I just am not sure what this changed and how. I am so deep in thought I never hear Kyle come into the bathroom.

"Morning beautiful," he says as he peers around the wall of the shower.

"Good morning to you, handsome," I say with a smile.

"I will make us some coffee and bring it back up while you get ready."

"Have I told you how wonderful you are lately?" I ask.

"Hmmm ... I 'm not sure, but I will never get tired of hearing it." He winks as he walks out.

When he comes back up with our coffee I am already blow-drying my hair. He puts the mugs on the counter and kisses my forehead. I love it when he does that. I watch him in the mirror as I continue to dry my hair. He has to be the sexiest man alive. I will never get tired of admiring him. When the sweat pants drop to the floor, my pulse quickens. I wonder if my body would have the same reactions to him if I didn't know him. I hear him laugh and realize I have just been staring at him. Oh well, he's mine and I can stare if I want to. So I smile at him and go back to my hair.

By the time Kyle and I pull up to KC's, my stomach is in knots. I am starting to think maybe this isn't such a good idea. As always, Kyle picks up on my anxiety and reaches for my hand.

"You'll be fine. There's nothing to be nervous about. It's just Beasley. He hasn't changed and neither have you." He squeezes my hand before he gets out of the truck. He comes around to my side and opens my door. I turn to get out, but he stops me.

"Maybe this will help." He grabs my face and pulls me to his lips, kissing me like it could be our last. Yeah, that helps. When we walk in Holly is behind the bar. She yells at us and nods over to a booth in the back. Beasley is sitting there tearing a napkin to shreds. At least I am not the only one who is nervous. For some reason that makes me feel so much better. I kiss Kyle's cheek and head over to the booth.

As soon as I get a foot away, Beasley clumsily stands up from the booth until I am seated across from him.

"Hi," I say and give him a small smile.

"Hi. I'm glad you wanted to meet me. I thought maybe you wouldn't want anything to do with me ever again," he says, nervously. I just jump in head-first. I tell him I was upset at first. Then I realized things were kept from me out of love and not to intentionally hurt me. I tell him I remember him going to every school function and every birthday party. He smiles as if remembering those things makes him happy. I figure I should get some of my questions out of the way.

"Did you love my mother?" I ask him but almost wish I hadn't when I see the look on his face. I'm not even sure how to describe it. It looks like a mixture of pain, sorrow, anger, and love all rolled up into one expression. It isn't pleasant. He has tears in his eyes as he speaks.

"I did. Hell, I still do. She is the only woman I have ever loved. There will never be anyone who can fill the hole I have in my heart from losing her." He chokes on his words a little. Wow. It has been twenty-three years, and he is still in love with her. Is that what it would be like if I lost Kyle or he lost me? God, I hope neither of us ever has to find out.

"Why didn't you tell me all of this at my grandparent's funeral? Why let me think I had no family, that I was all alone?" I ask him on the edge of my seat, waiting for an answer. This one is important. If he had told me, it could have changed so many things. For one, I would have known he was my father over a year ago. And two, I would have stayed here. That meant I would have been reunited with Kyle that much sooner.

"Amber, I am sorry I didn't tell you. You had just buried both of your grandparents. The two people you loved the most in this world … the ones who raised you. I didn't want to add to your grief or make you think any less of them. I swear, there is nothing I have wanted more than to tell you all these years. I just always thought it was better for you if I didn't, and the funeral just wasn't the right time." I can see the sincerity in his eyes.

"How does Beau know about my parents?

"When his parents died, he went to live with an aunt and uncle. His aunt was a nurse at the hospital where your mother was. It's the only explanation I can think of. I didn't want your grandparents' or parents' names to be tarnished, so my report said it was a carjacking gone wrong. Only a few people know the real story." We talk for a long time about everything and nothing. I tell him about my time in Atlanta and college. He asks some questions about the center. After a little while of chit-chat, I finally get the nerve to ask the big question I want to ask.

"There is one more thing I am wondering. It's kind of funny, really. I planned to ask you this before I knew you were my father. I was hoping... would you walk me down the aisle?" I ask nervously. He just sat there with his mouth hanging open. Oh no ... he didn't want to do it. I never thought he wouldn't want to. No, wait that's not it, he's shocked and emotional. His eyes are filling with tears. Before I realize what he's doing, he's on my side of the booth, hugging me so tightly I can't breathe. I start laughing because here's this big strong guy who carries a gun crying and hugging me like a girl. It's sweet but funny.

"Uh, Beasley I ... can't breathe ... too tight," I try to choke out. He quickly pulls back.

"I'm sorry. You really want me to walk you down the aisle? Like a real father does?" he asks, all excited like a kid at Christmas. I nod a yes and he smiles. It's contagious, so I smile back just as wide. Mistake. I am in another bone-crushing hug. Luckily, Kyle saves me this time. He comes over and taps Beasley on the shoulder.

"Do you mind not squeezing the air out of my girl? I would like to marry her in two weeks." He chuckles as he slides into the booth where Beasley had sat before he started hugging me to death. "It looks like your talk went well."

"I think it went very well. I will have the honor of walking this lovely woman down the aisle, and I couldn't be happier," Beasley says with a beaming smile. "I hate to leave so soon, but I do need to get back to the station. I will see you both later." He kisses my forehead and shakes Kyle's hand before he leaves.

Kyle

AMBER LOOKS so much happier than she was last night. I am thrilled that her talk with Beasley went well. I really hope they can get past all of this and have some kind of father-daughter relationship. We go sit up at the bar to eat some lunch and go over some more wedding details with Paul and Holly. They have both been such a huge help. I have a little thank you gift for them that is going to blow them away. As we all start eating, I figure it is the perfect time to give them their gift.

"Holly, remember when you said if my mom ever wanted to sell her house, to let you know?" I ask her. I watch as she and Paul perk up. They both have wanted to buy a house together, and they absolutely love my mom's house.

"Yes, is she putting up for sale?" she asks, all excited.

"Actually, she gave it to me. She decided to stay in Texas with my aunt, and she said I could do what I wanted with the house."

"So, are you going to sell it? How much?" I can see how much she wants the house.

"Amber and I were talking about it, and we decided we don't want to sell it." I see Holly go from excited to disappointed really quickly. I guess I picked on her long enough. "We decided we would rather just give it to a couple friends that we thought deserved it, because they are always doing so much for us." I watch her waiting for it to sink in. 3 ... 2 ... 1 ... and there it is. Holly runs around the bar and hugs me so tightly it almost knocks me off the stool. She finally lets go of me and moves on to Amber. Paul comes over and hugs me, too.

"Are you sure about this? That's a big thing to just give away," he asks.

"I am positive. I would rather my best friends be happy in a house I know they both love, than sell it to someone who doesn't really care about it. You guys have done so much for us, and we want to say thank you by giving you this house. Plus, Amber likes the fact that Holly will live in walking distance from her." I laugh.

"Well, how can I deny them a chance to live so close together?" Paul says with a chuckle.

I just can't believe this is my life. Everything seems so perfect. The bar is doing great, I will be marrying Amber soon, and I have great friends. I can't remember the last time I have felt this content and happy. And it's all because of the beautiful woman sitting next to me. Now, all I have to do is find Beau. Once Amber no longer has him to worry about, she will be a lot more relaxed, and frankly, so will I.

CHAPTER
Twenty-Two

Amber

"WAKE UP! Wake up!" Holly is yelling as she jumps up and down on my bed like a little kid. I open one eye to look at her, and she has a huge smile on her face. "Why are you not the one jumping with excitement? It is your wedding day, after all." She has her hands resting on her hips, and she's glaring at me.

"I am excited. I am just not awake." Plus, it felt like it took hours to get to sleep. At first I thought I was just too excited. You know, like when you were a kid on Christmas Eve. It's not that, though. The last couple of days I have had this really bad feeling. I just feel like something bad is going to happen. Maybe its normal wedding jitters, but I just don't think that's it. It could be that we haven't heard anything from or about Beau since he left the flowers at our house a couple weeks ago. The longer he goes without being arrested, the more nervous I get. I promised Holly last night that I wouldn't worry about anything at all today, so I am going to do my best not to.

"We have everything set up downstairs to do hair and make-up. I also have some food and coffee in the kitchen after you take your shower. Now, move it, lady, we don't have all day." She giggles and bounces back downstairs. I seriously love that girl.

I walk over to the window to see what is underway in the backyard. There are people moving around all over the place out there. The caterers are setting up their grills along with the tables to lay all of the food out on. All of the tables and chairs are being set up all around the back yard. The tables are round with plum, satin table cloths. The chairs have plum covers with a satin black sash on the back. The plates and cloth napkins are black. All of the glassware on the tables is crystal. They are gorgeous, glistening subtly in the sunlight. All of the center pieces are silk flower arrangements consisting of an array of purples and blacks. Holly and I had a difference of opinion when it came to all of this stuff. I wanted simple, something more like a barbecue. I wanted it to feel relaxed and laid back. All the beautiful things were her idea. I am so thankful that she talked me into it now. It's amazing. The ceremony itself is going to take place over by the pond. There is a small gazebo that hangs out over the water where we will be standing. We set up a few rows of chairs for all of our guests.

I head in to take a shower. As I'm getting dressed, my phone beeps with a text from Kyle.

> **Kyle:** *I really missed sleeping next to you last night. I can't wait to see you and make you my wife :)*
> **Me:** *I missed you last night, too. Me either. I love you :)*
> **Kyle:** *I love you, too xx*

All the guys stayed at Marcus's house and all of us girls stayed here. That, too, was Holly's idea. I thought Kyle was going to strangle her when she said I could not see him until I was walking down the aisle. I like that tradition. I think it adds to the anticipation and makes that moment when you start down the aisle and see each other more special. I still cannot believe in four more hours I will be Mrs. Kyle Connor. It seems like I have waited my whole life for today.

When I walk into the kitchen I am greeted with squeals and hugs from Taryn, Makenna, and Anna. Once they finish I am ambushed again by Beth and Pat who are here to do our make-up and hair. They own the only salon in town. I went to school with both of them, so I have known them for a while. They are really great girls. Holly has fresh fruit, croissants, and mimosas on the counter for breakfast. We all have so much fun while we are having our hair and make-up done.

I haven't laughed this hard in a very long time. Time is flying by so quickly. Before I know it, it's time to put my dress on.

I'm standing in front of the full-length mirror in our bedroom, and cannot believe it is my own reflection that I am seeing. It is all perfect; the dress, the hair, and the make-up. I look and feel like a princess. Holly comes in and stands behind me. I can see the tears building up in her eyes. If she starts crying, it will make me cry. I refuse to ruin my make-up.

"Don't you dare start crying, Holly," I scold her playfully.

"You look so beautiful. I am so happy for you and Kyle. You both deserve to be happy."

"Thank you for all of your help with the wedding and everything else that you do. I am so glad you're my friend." I wrap my arms around her in a hug.

"I am glad we are friends, too. Now, no more mushy stuff or we will both be bawling." As she steps back there is a knock at the bedroom door. Holly walks to the door and pokes her head out to see who it is. I turn around and see Beasley walk through the door. Holly says she needs to check on some things and she'll be back in a while.

"Wow. You look beautiful," he says as he kisses my cheek. These last couple of weeks we have spent a lot of time together. It hasn't been as difficult as I thought it would be to get used to the fact that he is my father. I haven't had any family in so long, it's nice to know that I have someone. He really is a good man and I'm very happy he's here with me today.

"You look pretty handsome yourself in that tux." He actually blushes. I never pictured him as the shy type. He acts like he isn't used to getting compliments. I can't imagine a handsome man like him doesn't have women falling all over themselves to get to him.

"Thank you. I have a couple things for you, do you have a few minutes?" I nod and smile. I'm afraid to talk. I'm so damn emotional and I refuse to cry until Kyle at least sees me first. Beasley pulls out a long, black velvet box from his inside his jacket.

"This was my mother's. She passed away before I knew you were my daughter. She would have loved you and you her. You look a lot like her. I'll have to show you some pictures sometime. I would like you to have this. Her mother gave it to her on her wedding day." He hands me the box. I open it to find the most exquisite diamond and amethyst bracelet. The style looks Victorian and so unique. I have never seen anything like it. Plus, it has amethysts in it, and I do love anything purple.

"It is amazing and gorgeous. It looks so old, it must have been in the family for a long time."

"From what I was told, it's from the late 1800's, and has been in the family as long. Someday you may have a daughter to pass it on to." I give him a huge hug. This is one of the most amazing gifts I have ever received. He lifts the bracelet out of the box and clasps it on my wrist. It looks even better on.

"Thank you. I love it, Dad." Wow. That was the first time I have called him dad, but it just felt right. Damn. I am going to have to touch-up my make-up.

"I love you, too. I like being called Dad," he says with a smile and teary eyes. "Okay, this is from your grandma. She gave it to me about six months before she passed away and asked me to give it to you on your wedding day. I will let you read it in private. See you in a little bit." He kisses my forehead and walks out the door. I am going to be emotionally exhausted before the wedding even starts. I miss my grandparents every day. Today, I have missed them more than usual. I never imagined this day without them. I take a deep breath and get my shaky hands to open the envelope. As soon as I unfold the paper and see her handwriting, I smile.

> *Dear Amber,*
>
> *I want to make sure you know we are with you on this special day, maybe not in body, but in spirit. You are so much more to us than just a granddaughter. You are the most precious gift we were ever given. You have always made us so very proud of you. I couldn't be happier that you and Kyle finally realized what all of the rest of us already knew, that the two of you were meant to be together. The two of you were in love long before either of you knew what love was. You probably think I'm crazy, writing this letter while you are engaged to someone other than Kyle not even living in the same state. Maybe I am, but I am pretty sure it is Kyle you are marrying today. Your grandfather and I both have loved Kyle like a grandson since we met him and have seen how much he loves you. We knew why you left to*

go to Atlanta, it's a small town and people talk. I never stuck my nose in it except the once to tell him where you lived. Unfortunately, that wasn't the right time for the two of you either. You make sure to tell him how happy we are that he is part of our family and to take care of our baby. Tell him that we love him and always have.

I am also sure by now Beasley has told you about your parents. Amber, we can't apologize enough for how we handled that. At first, we just weren't thinking clearly. We had just found out about the affair and that Charles wasn't your biological father. Of course that part didn't matter to us where you were concerned. We loved you and you were our granddaughter, biology had nothing to do with that. We loved your mother. She was hurting and our son was hurting. You'll see one day when you have children, when they hurt, you hurt. Then, he did the most unthinkable thing imaginable to me. I hate what he did to your mother and to himself, but I loved my son. It was so confusing for me, the different emotions all bombarding me at once. I hated the monster that would so coldly take the life of the woman he loved, then so cowardly take his own. But, I loved the son that I raised. The one that was always sweet, gentle, kind, and loving. He was head over heels in love with your mother. And you, my dear, had him wrapped around your tiny little finger. I was so torn with my feelings. When I would grieve for my son, I would feel so much guilt. It is an unbearable feeling to love and hate your own child in equal amounts. If it wasn't for you, I don't think your grandfather and I would have survived. You gave us hope, love, and happiness. Part of not telling you was selfish and for that, I am truly sorry. I was afraid if you knew our son was such a monster you wouldn't want to be anywhere near us. Beasley is a good man. I hope you are giving him a chance. He wanted to tell you that he was your father. I think he loved and respected us too much to ever push us on it, though. We have apologized to him for not allowing him to be the father he should have been for all those years. I hope someday you can forgive us and know that we never intended to hurt you in anyway.

Please, always remember that we love you more than anything in this world. You have made our lives so wonderful. We are so proud of the strong, smart, beautiful, and loving woman you have grown to be. We will always be with you, watching over you, and loving you especially today. We love you, Amber.
Love Always and Forever,
Grandma and Grandpa

Yeah, I am definitely going to need a touch up for my face. I can't imagine what they must have gone through when Charles killed my mother and himself. You would never have known that my grandparents had been through that kind of heartache and agony. They were always such happy, sweet, and loving people. I didn't just save them, I think we saved each other. I mean Beau went through the same thing with his parents and look at the kind of monster he turned out to be. Just the thought of him brings back that dreaded feeling in the pit of my stomach. I am not going to feel like that today. I will worry about him and his craziness after our wedding. I still can't believe that my grandmother had so much faith that Kyle and I would end up together, even when I was engaged to Daniel. It would have been a little embarrassing if I wasn't marrying Kyle. I am laughing at that thought when all of the girls walk in for last minute touch-ups. Thank God because I really need one. It's almost time.

Kyle

I AM sitting on the front porch of the house trying to keep myself from going to see Amber. I hated not being with her last night and not waking up with her this morning. The front door opens and Beasley walks out.

"Mind if I join you for a minute?" he asks as he motions to the chair beside me.

"No, not at all. Have you seen Amber yet?" I ask.

"I have, you are one very lucky man. She is the most beautiful bride I have ever seen, and I'm not just saying that because she's my daughter," he says with a chuckle and a beaming smile. It is so easy to see how much he loves her, how proud he is to be her father. I am so glad he told her the truth about everything. She has handled it all in true Amber fashion, just like I thought she would. They have spent quite a bit of time together the last few weeks and they seem to be really bonding.

"Believe me, I know how lucky I am to have her in my life. She is an amazing person. I am going to do my damnedest every day to make her as happy as she makes me."

"There is no doubt in my mind of that, Son. As long as you love her, she'll be happy. I have something for you." He hands me a white sealed envelope with my name handwritten on the front. I look at it carefully. It looks like Ima's handwriting.

"Ima gave it to me about six months before she passed away. She told me to give it to you on your wedding day." He laughs and shakes his head. "The day you and Amber got married. That woman always swore up and down it would happen, they are fated to be together was what she always said. I'll let you read it, I have to go check on Amber." He pats me on the back and goes back in the house. I open the letter and begin to read it.

> Dear Kyle,
>
> I am so happy for you today. I have always known in my heart this day would come. You and Amber were meant to be together, I told you that when you came to me wanting to know how to find her. Gene and I couldn't be happier that you are the man she will be spending the rest of her life with. We have always loved you like you were our own grandson, and now you are. We are very proud of the man you have become. I know you will take care of our granddaughter and treasure her like the precious gift that she is.
>
> I imagine it wasn't easy on her when she learned the truth about her parents, but with such a loving, caring man by her side, I am sure it was much more bearable. For that, I thank you. Beasley is a good man, and he loves Amber very much. I hope neither of you hold any

of this against him. He wanted to tell her the truth so many times, but respected our wishes not to.

We never told her because we thought we were protecting her. I hope you both know we would never intentionally do anything to hurt either of you.

We are with you both today and always in spirit. We love you both very much, and are at peace knowing the two of you are finally together, making one another happy.

Love always and forever,
Grandma and Grandpa

And here I didn't think today could get any better. I have always thought of them as my grandparents. I never knew any of mine and they always treated me the same way they did Amber. They were amazing people. I really loved them both and I miss them so much every day. I hope Amber is okay, I am sure Ima had a similar letter for her today, as well. Not having her grandparents here today will be the hardest thing for her. At least now she has Beasley. Unfortunately, my mother is too sick to travel, so she won't be here today. I told her not to worry, that we would come to visit her soon. Nothing is going to ruin how happy I am today. I get to marry the girl of my dreams, my true love, my soul mate. What could be better than that? I put the letter in my jacket pocket and start heading out toward the pond. It's show time!

CHAPTER
Twenty-Three

Amber

I CAN'T WAIT to see Kyle. We are all lined up just out of sight from everyone, waiting for the music to start. I am nervous, but it's an excited nervousness. The music starts and Makenna starts walking, followed by Taryn, then Holly. They all look so beautiful. We chose silk flowers for the bouquets so that they would last forever. The girls' bouquets are made of three purple and three black roses. Mine is made with six purple and six white roses. I hear the wedding march start to play. Beasley hooks my arm through his and smiles down at me.

"You ready?" he asks.

"More than ever," I tell him with a smile, and we start walking. As soon as we round the corner and I lock eyes with Kyle, everything else around me fades away. Everything I will ever need for the rest of my life is standing there at the end of this aisle smiling at me. That smile makes my knees weak. He is more handsome than usual standing there in that tux. It looks really good on him. When we reach Kyle, Beasley kisses my cheek and takes his seat. I hand my bouquet to Holly. Kyle takes my hands in his, leans in close to me, and whispers, "You are the most beautiful woman I have ever seen. You take my breath away,

Princess." I just smile at him. The lump in my throat is so big there is no way I can say a word.

The ceremony itself is short. I hate going to weddings and having to sit for over an hour through a boring ceremony. I swore I wasn't doing that to our friends. We are going with the traditional vows. When the pastor says the magic words, you may kiss the bride, a huge grin comes across Kyle's face. He wraps me in his arms and kisses me like we are the only two here. In that moment, I don't care, though. When we finally break apart, we realize everyone is clapping and cheering. All of the guests head over to where we have everything set up for the reception while we stay to have some pictures taken. I notice my dad leaving toward the reception.

"Um ... Dad, aren't you going to stay and get in some pictures?" He has a surprised look on his face. I'm not sure if it is because I ask or because he doesn't want to be in the pictures.

"It's okay if you don't want to," I say nervously.

"No, I would love to. You have just pleasantly surprised me twice today by calling me Dad," he says as he hugs me. Here I am, standing between the love of my life and my dad. I don't think I have ever been this happy. We spend the next hour taking so many pictures my cheeks are sore from smiling.

By the time we make it to where everyone else is, I'm starving. Kyle did an excellent job choosing a caterer. This is the best food I have ever had. The fact that it is all my favorites helped a little, too. After we finish eating, Kyle introduces me to the guys from Deuce.

"Guys, this is my beautiful wife, Amber. Amber this is Jake, Devlin, Cameron, and Logan." They all smile. Each of them stands and, one by one, come over to kiss my cheek and say hello. They are all very nice, not to mention gorgeous. I can just imagine the line of women that would be around when Kyle's band and these guys were all out together. Jake, Devlin, and Cameron are brothers. They are almost identical. They are tall with long blond hair. Their eyes are baby blue and they have deep, dark California tans. They remind me of surfers. Poor Logan sticks out like a sore thumb next to these three. He has dark brown hair, brown eyes, and is much shorter. The only thing in common, aside from being handsome, is that he also has the deep, dark tan.

Once everyone finishes eating, Kyle and I have our first dance. I am in heaven. We chose the song he sang to me the day he proposed, *Tangled Up In You* by Staind. I love this song. He holds me close and softly sings it to me in my ear. How could I not be in love with this man? I can't wait to get this reception over with and take my husband to bed. My husband. I love saying that.

"Was it everything you wanted, Princess?" he asks as he kisses me sweetly.

"No. It was so much better than I could have ever dreamed it to be. I still cannot believe we are married."

"I know, it feels like I am in the middle of the best dream I have ever had. Promise me, if this is a dream, don't ever wake me up. I have never been this happy and it's all because of you."

"It's all real. I have never been this happy, either. I never thought it was even possible. It just keeps getting better every day," I say, then kiss him. Every time I think of how happy we are, I can't help but think there is something waiting to take it all away. That something is Beau. I know it is just a matter of time before he resurfaces again.

After our dance, I dance with my dad. It still feels so weird to call him my dad. After all these years, it is weird to know I still have a dad that is alive. Beasley is all smiles for the entire dance.

When it is time to cut the cake, Kyle and I stand by the cake and everyone gathers around us. The cake we chose has four tiers and is in the shape of a heart. It is purple with white pearls around each tier. Kyle stands behind me as we cut into the cake together. I place a slice on the plate. This is the moment of truth. What is he going to do? Is he going to be nice when he feeds me a bite? He picks the slice of cake up and slowly brings it to my lips. I take a bite. It is awesome cake. Before he puts it back down, he runs the slice of cake along the tip of my nose, then quickly licks the tiny bit of frosting off. Oh, I couldn't wait for the honeymoon to begin. I pick up the rest of the cake and bring it to his mouth. Just as he closes his eyes, I smash it all over his lips. Everyone starts laughing. I try to run, but Kyle grabs me.

"You're not getting away that easily, Princess." He laughs as he crashes his cake-covered lips to mine.

"Mmm ... raspberry." I laugh and kiss him again. When we finally come up for air, I notice I have frosting on my dress. I tell Kyle I am going inside for a minute to clean it off. He jokes and says if I am not back in five minutes he is coming to find me.

Everyone is out back, so the house is quiet when I walk in. I go to the kitchen and wet a towel in the sink. As I am wiping the cake from my dress, I feel someone come up behind me.

"Babe, it hasn't been five minutes, yet. Do you miss me already?" I joke. As soon as he speaks my blood turns cold.

"Of course I've missed you, Amber. Every single second we have been apart," Beau says, trying to sound sweet. I feel the gun poke into my back.

"You and I are going for a little ride. I suggest you be very quiet unless you want someone to get hurt," he says as he grabs my arm. He starts to pull me toward the front door. I am not going to do this again. I try to pull out of his hold, but his grip on me is too tight. I see a glass on the counter. I grab it and throw it toward the window, then everything goes black.

Kyle

PAUL AND I are standing by the back door talking when, all of a sudden, we hear a glass break. We run into the kitchen, but no one is there. I look down on the floor and see a couple spots of blood. I panic. Paul is looking out the window.

"Oh, shit! He's got her ... let's go!" Paul yells and starts for the front door. I turn and look out of the window so I can see what in the hell he is talking about. In one split second, my whole world is being ripped away. Beau is putting a lifeless Amber into a truck. I somehow get myself moving and follow Paul. By the time we get outside, Beau is already leaving down the driveway. Paul unlocks his truck and we jump in to follow. He calls Beasley to fill him in. Within a few minutes, his car is behind us, lights and sirens blaring. I can't take my eyes off of the truck, finding anything to focus on instead of my thoughts and shaky hands.

I look over at Paul and see he is concentrating on the road intently. As I watch Beau's truck, I get more nervous. The faster we go, the more dangerous and careless Beau seems to drive. I realize that when he put Amber in the truck, he didn't buckle her in. I can't lose her; I just fucking married her. Please, don't let me lose her.

Everything that happens next seems to be in slow motion. I glance at the speedometer and see that we are going about 95 MPH, which means Beau is going much faster. We are coming up to a fairly busy intersection. I see Amber sit up in the passenger seat. It looks like she is trying to open her door. Beau turns to look at her taking his attention away from the road. Our light turns red, but Beau isn't facing the road. Paul hits the brakes hard as Beasley skids to a stop next to us. The brake lights ahead of us never come on. Just as he reaches the center of the intersection a tractor-trailer slams into the driver's side of Beau's truck. The sound of the metal crunching and glass breaking pierces my ears. I see Beau's truck flying in the air and landing on the passenger side. I don't even realize I am out of Paul's truck until I feel his arms around me trying to keep me from flinging myself at the wreckage. The truck is unrecognizable. The cab is totally crushed. The paramedics, fire department, and most of the sheriff's department have already arrived. Beasley must have already called to have them on standby.

I keep looking around, praying to see Amber walk away safe and sound, but that never happens. The exact time Paul lets go of me, I spot her. She is lying about twenty feet away from the truck. My God, my Princess is lying in the middle of the road, still in her wedding dress. I take off running and manage to get to her before anyone stops me. She isn't moving and she's covered in blood. I slowly reach for her hand.

"Please, Princess hang on. Don't leave me please." I am crying, begging. "Princess ... you need to be okay. We have a honeymoon to take. We haven't even had a wedding night." I try anything I can to get some kind of reaction from her. I can't lose her, I just can't.

"Come on, Kyle. Give the paramedics some room so they can help her," Paul says as he pulls me up and moves me back a little. I fall to my knees and cry. I can't stop. Not knowing if she is okay is crushing me. Paul is right beside me, comforting me as best he can.

"She has to be okay, Paul. I can't survive without her. Please tell me she'll be okay." I am still sobbing, but I don't give a shit about what I look like right now. The only thing in the world that I care about is lying on the pavement, and I don't know if she is alive or dead.

What feels like hours, but is only moment, pass before I notice Beasley next to us looking just as bad as I probably did. I grab his hand and hold it tightly. He is the only one who has any idea what I am feeling right now. He just got her in his life, too. This isn't fair. She didn't do anything to deserve this. Why is this happening to her? To us?

"We have a pulse, but it's weak. We have to go now," I hear the paramedic say. Oh, thank God. At least she's breathing. I stand up. I am going in that ambulance with her. I am not leaving her side. She needs me, needs to know I am right here with her. I really don't know what I would do without Paul. He is always so calm and level-headed. He knows what I am thinking before I even open my mouth.

"You ride with Amber. I will go back to the house and take care of the guests. We will be at the hospital as soon as we can. Will you be okay?" Paul asks. Before I can answer, Beasley cuts in.

"He won't be alone. I will follow the ambulance to the hospital. I'll be there with him. Go ahead and take care of the house, and we will meet you there. Don't worry, Paul, I'll watch out for my son-in-law," he says with a sad smile. Paul nods to Beasley and squeezes my shoulder. I watch him get in his truck and drive off toward my house.

By the time we reach the hospital, Amber had stopped breathing three times. The injury they are most worried about at the moment is her head injury. Apparently she was thrown head-first through the windshield. As we enter the emergency room, a nurse hands me a clipboard. She tells me to sit in the waiting area and fill out the paperwork, and they will let me know something as soon as the doctors have any news. As much as I don't want to leave her, I know I have no choice.

"Come on, son. Let's go have a seat. I'll help ya fill that shit out," Beasley says as he guides me to the waiting area. We sit down and start on the paperwork, hoping it will help pass some of the time. About forty minutes later, Paul and a very hysterical Holly walk in. I explain that the only thing we have been told so far is that she is in surgery. She has bleeding as well as major swelling in her brain. They are trying to stop the bleeding in surgery. It isn't long before the waiting room begins to fill up. Jax, Leena, Marcus, Angel, Clark, Marty, Anna, Taryn, and even Jake, Devlin, Cameron, and Logan are here. So many people are praying for her; she has to pull through.

"Hey," Marcus says as he puts an arm around me. "Mr. and Mrs. Thompson are handling the clean-up at the house. Makenna and Matthew are watching all of the kids, so we are all here for you for as long as you need us."

"Thank you." I can't think of anything other than Amber right now. The doctors tell us her condition is very critical. Even if they stop the bleeding, the swelling may not go down. He tells me to be prepared for the possibility that she may not make it through this. There is no way to prepare for that. I can't live without her.

CHAPTER
Twenty-Four

Kyle

WE ALL wait at the hospital for hours without saying much. What is there to say? There is nothing we can say to comfort each other. I know the only thing that will bring me any comfort is to hear that Amber will be perfectly fine. I look up at the clock. We haven't seen or heard from a doctor in almost five hours. I don't know how much more of this not knowing I can stand. I stand up, walk to the window, and look at the moon. Amber always loved sitting outside at night, staring up at the sky. Just the other night we laid out by the pond looking at the stars discussing our future. I thought at the time that our future was as bright as the stars, but now I am not so sure. She was so excited when I asked her if we could try to start a family soon. When I mentioned it, I was worried that she would want to wait a year or two, but as always, she was right there on the same page. It feels like all my dreams are slowly slipping through my fingers and I can't do a damn thing to stop it. That son of a bitch took everything from us.

I have been so worried about Amber that I totally forgot all about Beau. I don't even know what happened to him, not that I care as long as the police have him. I motion for Beasley to come over. I have to know where Beau is.

"You okay? Do you need something?" Beasley asks. He looks as bad as I am sure I do right now.

"Where is the asshole that did this to my wife? I just want five minutes with him," I say, trying to control my temper.

"Unfortunately, you won't get your five minutes with him, but I have a feeling where he is right now is much worse than anything you and I could give him." I give him a confused look. What could be worse for Beau than me getting my hands on him?

"Where is he, Beasley?" I am getting frustrated now. I am too emotional for guessing games.

"He died on impact, so I would assume Beau had a one way ticket to the gates of Hell. Believe me, like you, I wish I could have been the one to send him there, but he's there all the same," he says without an ounce of remorse, not that I had any either. He is right. If Beau hadn't died, I probably would've killed him if I had gotten my hands on him. At least I knew he could never hurt Amber again.

"Mr. Connor." I look up to see a doctor in green scrubs. He doesn't look like he has good news. I'm not sure if I want to know what he has to say. I take a deep breath and slowly walk over to where he stands.

"I'm Kyle Connor. How's my wife?" I ask. My stomach twists in knots.

"We were able to stop the bleeding, but there is still a great deal of swelling. The next few days are critical. She is still in a coma at this point, which is best," he states.

"Will she be okay?" I ask.

"I honestly can't answer that. It can go either way, at this point. There is a possibility that she may never wake up. There is also a possibility that if she does wake up, there could be significant brain damage. She could also wake up and be perfectly fine. We just have no way of knowing, especially this early. We just need to wait and see how she does. I wish I could give you something more. I promise you … we are doing everything we can for your wife."

"Can I see her now?" I ask. I need to see her, to hold her hand, so she knows I am with her. I want her to fight as hard as she can to come back to me.

"Let us get her settled in ICU. A nurse will come get you in a little while." He gives me a sympathetic look and leaves the way he came. I tell everyone they should go home and rest, that if anything changes

I will call right away. Everyone but Paul, Marcus, Angel, and Beasley agree, but say they are coming back tomorrow morning. Holly is reluctant, but somehow Paul convinces her it is for the best. When they all leave, the rest of us move to the waiting room upstairs for the ICU.

"Mr. Connor, you can go in and see your wife now," an older nurse says with a sweet smile. I turn and see Paul and Beasley exchange looks before Paul is at my side.

"Can I go with him, just in case?" He gives the nurse a look that says, "Just in case he falls apart." She smiles at him and nods her head, then leads us to Amber's room.

The moment I see her laying in that bed, all of the air is knocked out of me and I feel my legs give out. Luckily, Paul is right there. He grabs me and keeps me from falling down. She looks so broken and battered. Her head is all bandaged up. There is a tube that helps her breathe. I sit in the chair Paul slides next to her bed and I reach for her hand, bringing it to my lips. I don't realize I am crying until I notice the tears falling onto her hand.

"Princess, I don't know if you can hear me, but if you can, I love you with everything that I am. I need you to fight as hard as you can and come back to me. We just started. Our story can't end like this, it's not how we planned it." I can't hold it in any longer. I hold her hand to my lips and cry. Paul's hand grips my shoulder to let me know he is there.

The first week goes by with some change in Amber's condition. The swelling in her brain is going down, but she is still in a coma. I have refused to leave her side for more than five minutes since she has been here. I know everyone is trying to help me by getting me out of this room, but I am afraid she'll wake up and I won't be there. I have probably lost ten pounds, not on purpose. I just can't make myself eat much. I sleep in the chair pushed next to her bed so I can hold her hand. When I'm able to sleep, anyway. Beasley is here almost as much as I am. Paul, Marcus, Angel, Holly, and Taryn come and go in shifts. They always try to make me eat, and when I don't, they try to guilt me into it by saying I need to stay healthy for Amber. They eventually get me to take a bite or two, and then leave me alone.

By week three I am about to lose my fucking mind. I am lost without her, and every day that goes by I feel like she is slipping away from me. I talk to her all the time, begging her to come back to me, telling her how much I love and need her, but nothing is working. The good news is that all of the swelling is gone and she is out of danger. Last night, they moved her to a private room, so she is no longer in ICU. Paul had brought my acoustic by for me this morning. I figured I've tried everything else, maybe singing to her might help.

"Princess, I heard this song a while back and it made me think of how I feel about you. It's called *I Will Be* by Leona Lewis. I hope you like it." I pick up my guitar and softly play.

"That was beautiful, Kyle." I look up and see Holly with tears streaming down her face. "Sorry, I didn't mean to interrupt."

"It's okay. I'm hoping music will help since nothing else seems to," I say sadly as I put the guitar back in its case.

"I wouldn't be too sure of that," Holly says with excitement. When I turn around, I see Amber's eyes fluttering open. Holly runs past me, saying she is getting a nurse. I go right to Amber's side and hold her hand. She looks a little panicked and grabs for the tube in her mouth. I try to calm her as best I can, but the way she looks at me is almost like she has no idea who I am.

"Amber, sweetie, calm down. That tube is there to help you breathe. The nurse will be in any minute." I am still holding her hand, but the look in her eyes is really scaring me. The doctor comes in followed by a couple of nurses. He asks Holly and me to wait in the waiting area so he can remove the tube and examine Amber fully.

"Princess, I'll be right outside if you need me. I love you," I say as I kiss her head. As soon as we get to the waiting room, we both start calling everyone we know to tell them the good news. For the first time in three weeks, my heart doesn't hurt. I'm happy again. My Princess is awake. I want so badly to hold her in my arms.

It doesn't take long for the waiting room to fill up will all of our friends. About an hour later, the nurse comes out and asks Beasley and me to come back to the room. When I walk in, I smile at Amber, but she looks away from me. Something is very wrong, I'm not sure what it is, but I think we are about to find out. I look over at Beasley and he has a very uneasy look on his face.

"I have checked Amber over and, physically, everything looks great," he says. He takes a deep breath, then continues, "There is one problem, however. At this point, we have no way of knowing if it is temporary or permanent." If this fucking doctor doesn't just spit it out, I am going to strangle him. "Amber has complete amnesia. She doesn't remember anything or anyone. She doesn't even know who she is." I look over at Amber and she is just staring down at her hands in her lap. I knew by the way she looked at me when she woke up something was wrong, but this I don't think I can handle. What if it's permanent? There is a chance she may never remember who I am. I have to get out of here; it feels like the walls are closing in on me. My chest feels tight and I can't breathe. I push past Beasley and out the door. As I am passing the waiting room, Paul grabs me.

"What's going on? What happened?" I know he's concerned, but I can't even think. I hurt too badly.

"She doesn't remember anything. Not. A. Fucking. Thing. She doesn't even know her own name. I can't take this right now, I have to get the hell out of here." I pull my arm away, but he stops me again.

"Here. You don't have any way to leave. Just be careful, and when I call later to check on you, please answer so I don't worry," he says as he hands me the keys to his truck.

"Thanks," is all I can say. I get out of the hospital as fast as I can. When I get in the truck, I think about where to go. I can't go home. There are too many memories and I can't deal with that now. The bar, that's where I need to go. I need to drink until I can't feel this pain anymore. Tonight, I forget. Tomorrow, I will try to figure out how to get my girl back.

THE END

Acknowledgments

I want to thank most of all my husband John and son Cody. You both have had to deal with my reading obsession and now my writing obsession as well. This is something I have always wanted to do, but never had the courage, but with your love and support I found the courage. I love you both more than you'll ever know.

To all the rest of my family. (There are way too many of you to thank individually) Thank you for all of your support and encouragement. I love all of you very much.

Thank you to all of the ladies that were beta readers. You all are awesome, I really enjoyed working with you on this book. I look forward to working with you on book two.

Thank you Becky Schmidt for all of the help you have given me. You have no idea how much it is appreciated. I am so glad our paths crossed.

Susan Taylor Arden, I can't begin to thank you enough. I appreciate all of the help and guidance you have given me.

Monica Black what can I say...you are my hero!

Contact Author

Kathy-Jo would love to hear from you:

Facebook www.facebook.com/authorkathyjoreinhart
Twitter twitter.com/KathyJoReinhart
Website kathyjoreinhart.com
Goodreads www.goodreads.com/author/show/7890595.Kathy_Jo_Reinhart

First Love Playlist

Breathing Slowly - Crossfade
I'll Fight - Daughtry
From Where You Are - Lifehouse
Die For You - Otherwise
I Remember You - Skid Row
Believe - Staind
Gone Forever - Three Days Grace
Broken - Seether (Featuring Amy Lee)
Tangled Up In You - Staind
The Reason - Hoobastank
I Will Be - Leona Lewis

This paperback interior was designed and formatted by

www.emtippettsbookdesigns.com

Artisan interiors for discerning authors and publishers.